The Illusion of Us

Magnolia Farran

DragonFlute Press™

Publish by DragonFlute Press™
Spotsylvania, Virginia

ISBN: 979-8-9987622-0-8

First Edition

Printed in the United States of America

For inquiries, contact: www.dragonflutepress.com

Chapter 1

Owen stood in front of the bathroom mirror, enjoying the calm and quiet of the dark, cloudy morning. He took his time brushing his hair before dragging his feet to the square window. He put the brush handle in his mouth and pushed the window up, letting the cold air flood the small room.

"Stupid fall, it's so cold my body's going to turn to ice." Owen mumbled before taking the brush out of his mouth. He placed the brush on the black marble counter before walking out the bathroom door. Owen started walking to his bedroom when he heard faint tapping. He paused for a few seconds and looked around. After a second, he shrugged. "It's probably nothing." He told himself. When he opened his bedroom door he saw where the tapping was coming from. He was faced with Jake gripping the window frame with white papers hanging from his mouth. Owen stood there, his arms folded and a smug smirk on his face. He let Jake stand on the ladder in the cold for a few seconds before deciding to let him in.

"DUDE! It's *freezing* out here!" Jake exclaimed, tumbling through the window onto the carpeted floor as Owen tried his best to shush him. "Why did you just *stand* there?!" He asked more quietly as he picked himself off the floor.

"I need a reason?" Owen asked and nudged him playfully before taking the papers out of his mouth. "These the test papers?" He flipped the subject.

"Yep." Jake answered, walking over to the bed and flopping down. "My cousin apparently never throws things away. And our math teacher never makes up new tests." He added. Owen looked over the paper, his eyes lingering on the red ink that marked the test an A+.

"Are your parents up?" Jake questioned as he stood up after walking to the door, then glanced at the hallway.

Owen shrugged. "They should be."

"Good, cuz' I'm hungry." Jake walked out into the hallway and into the living room.

Owen followed closely behind, but left the test inside his room. "I'm guessing that means your parents weren't home today like they said?" He pondered.

"Yeah, but mom said they'll be home by Friday." Jake answered before adding. "Well, *should*. You know how they are" He shrugged as they turned into the kitchen.

Both of them were met with the overwhelming smell of bacon and the sizzling sound of it just hitting the pan. Their mouths started to water before Owen's dad started talking.

"Morning Owen, morning Jake. You know you can just come through the front door. You know where the key is." His father explained, not looking up from the pan now full with bacon and its popping grease.

"But where's the fun in that Mr. Eric?" Jake asked, making Owen's dad chuckle.

"I guess there isn't." Eric replied, smiling.

2

"Owen, dear, why was the window open in the bathroom?" His mother appeared from behind them, scooching past to stand at the island across from the stove.

Owen paused, his eyebrows furrowing slightly as he opened his mouth to respond. "Uh..." He mumbled, his face twisting into more confusion. "I don't know." He shrugged as he walked over to sit down beside his mom.

"Miss. Mary, are you driving Owen to school today? Cuz if so..."

"No, he's taking the bus today. I have a work thing in a few minutes." She answered before grabbing the half-loaf of bread from the refrigerator. "Feel free to eat anything though."

"Ok." Jake sat down at the counter, grabbed a banana from a bowl of fruits, peeled it, and started eating it.

"Did you two study for that test today?" She asked while placing two slices of bread into the toaster oven.

"Yep, and I'm going to get an A, like always." Jake mentioned, straightening his back slightly before taking another bite of the banana.

Owen scoffed and rolled his eyes. "Yeah. Sure." He replied sarcastically.

His mother snickered and turned back around to grab something from the refrigerator.

"Is it going to be like the "A" you got last week?" Owen questioned in a murmur as he smirked.

"*Duuude.*" Jake hissed, begging him with his eyes to stop talking.

Owen nudged him with his elbow. "Relax dude."

The sizzling bacon sound faded and Eric turned to reveal a full plate of cooked bacon. "Who wants-"

"ME!" Jake blurted out as he grabbed five whole slices in a single swipe of his hand.

"Save some for the rest of us Jake." Mary took two pieces and put them on a plate. The toaster oven then dinged and Mary grabbed the wooden tongs next to it to take out the toast. Owen watched as his mom put down peanut butter and jam on her toast.

"Ok, I'm off to work." Mary kissed Eric on the cheek, then pecked Owen on his forehead. "Goodbye my three handsome gentlemen." She said while giving Jake a side hug before walking down the other hallway toward the entrance.

"Bye Mom!" "Bye Honey!" "Bye Miss. Mary." The three of them called after her before hearing the front door shut.

"Owen, do you want anything? You haven't eaten yet." Eric asked, slightly concerned. He pushed the bacon plate closer to him.

"No, I'm not hungry." Owen answered. "I'll just grab something at school."

"Wow. You're not hungry? Really? That's *so* unlike you." Jake teased, taking a bite of two bacon strips.

Owen jabbed Jake in the side while he wasn't looking.

"Gah-." Jake rubbed his side while glaring at Owen.

"Ok boys, it's 6:40. The bus should be here by now." Eric said, trying to persuade them outside.

"Alright, I'll get my stuff." Owen sighed, standing up to head to his room.

"Yeah, me too." Jake stood up and followed him.

Once they turned the corner, Jake whispered into Owen's ear. "Dude, don't forget the test papers."

"I won't dude, relax. Take a chill pill."

4

"I will once those papers are in your bag." Jake grumbled and sped past Owen to get to his room first. Owen grabbed his bag as Jake snatched the papers off his bed. Owen grabbed the papers from him and shoved them into his backpack.

"Don't rip them!" Jake yelped and put his hands close to Owen's bag like he was about to catch it in case it fell.

"If you're so worried about the papers then you put them in there." Owen snapped, handing his bag to Jake and turning to put on his shoes.

"Boys! It'll leave if you don't get out here soon!" Eric shouted from the front porch.

"We're coming!" Owen screamed back, hopping on one foot as he struggled to get his last shoe on.

"I got your bag dude." Jake slid past him as Owen jumped into the hall and quickly sprinted behind him.

"Love you dad! Bye!" Owen jumped down the two porch steps and landed right beside Jake on the sidewalk.

"Bye boys!" Eric shouted, watching them chaotically sprint to the bus stop at the end of the sidewalk.

"We're here!" Owen panted, planting his hand on the bus stop sign post to catch his breath before climbing into the schoolbus. Jake slid slightly, almost losing his balance before stepping on.

"Just in time, as usual." The bus lady exasperated in her usual shrill and flat tone as they both went to sit down.

- - - - - - - - - -

The bus rolled down the decline and into the bus

loop where kids were already swarming the high school entrance.

"Ok, everyone off." The bus lady announced to the small group on the bus as the doors hissed open. Everyone filed out of the bus slowly and groggily.

Jake and Owen climbed down the surprisingly steep steps and onto the sidewalk. Jake huddled close to Owen as they walked forward. "Alright, we have until third period to have this memorized. So we should-"

"Wait." Owen stopped Jake with an outstretched arm. "Where did everyone go?" They both swiveled their heads around, slowly stepping backward and looking around everywhere. The usual noise of crazy, sleep deprived teens disappeared as quickly as it started. A sharp stinging wind hit them as they turned back to each other.

"And the buses?" Jake added, prompting Owen to turn to the bare bus loop.

Dark, ominous clouds swarmed the sky, making the situation more frightening. Both of them slowly walked back to each other with their eyes on the sky.

"Let's go inside." Jake proposed, though his voice wavered.

"Yep." Owen agreed, his heartbeat slowly quickening as they walked.

Their shoes echoed through the halls inside. Both of them walked through the deserted halls together, brushing shoulders with each step.

"This is so weird dude. What are we going to do?" Owen murmured to Jake.

"Why do you think *I* know what to do?" Jake murmured back.

A classroom door creaked open behind them.

Both of them whirled around to face the sound, jumping out of their skin at the suddenness.

"Boys?" Their math teacher approached them. "What are you doing here?"

"Hello sir. We're here for school." Jake replied, recovering quickly.

"But it's a Saturday?" The teacher informed them with a confused tone. He folded his arms, waiting for a better excuse.

"No... it's Tuesday." Jake insisted, shifting his feet while gripping Owen's backpack.

Owen grabbed his phone out of his back pocket. "Look sir, see it's-" He froze, seeing bright saturated colors where his phone should have been. He instinctively threw it and let the colorful brick hit the floor, taking two steps back.

"Dude what was- woah." Jake's eyes widened when he looked down at the phone.

Their teacher bent down and picked it up. "Look right here, it says-" Static followed, probably the date.

Owen took a step back, his hands trembling as he tensed up.

"Dude. Breathe." Jake urged and placed a hand on Owen's shoulder.

Owen took a deep breath as he closed his eyes, hoping it would all disappear. "Let's get out of here."

The school bell let out a deafening ring, and a second later the classroom doors swung open. Owen gasped and froze, unsure of what to do.

"This is getting super freaky dude." Jake grabbed Owen's wrist and pulled them out of the hallway to the front doors. They felt people around them and heard muffled voices, like being underwater. He pushed the front door open and everything seemed normal again.

"Huh." Jake uttered. "What do we do now?" He let go of Owen's wrist and turned to face him.

"I-I... don't know. Let's go home?" Owen stammered, wiping his sweaty palms on his jeans, still shaken from the incident.

"Uhh... ok. We just need to find a car or something?" Jake mumbled to himself, but loud enough to let Owen here.

A few seconds passed, letting Owen soak in most of what happened. Half of him thought he was still asleep. He couldn't be though right? "Oh, there!" Jake exclaimed, shaking Owen out of his trance. "I can drive this." Jake explained, leading Owen to a tall, dinged up, four-door truck.

"Ok." Owen said, still in his dazed state. Jake hoisted himself up into the driver's side and Owen got in on the passenger's side. Owen closed his door last and the engine revved to life.

"Wow. Magic car!" Jake's eyes widened with surprise and excitement as he gripped the steering wheel. Owen had thought nothing of it until Jake said something, but by the time he put two and two together, they were off. Owen started to calm down, looking out at the bare trees and the leaves scattered on the ground before he realized.

"Wait. You have your license?" He asked, turning to look at Jake, who was gripping the wheel so hard his somewhat tan skin turned white. Jake didn't look at Owen.

"Ehhhh..."

"Do you at least have your permit?"

"MMMMMHHH"

"DUDE!" Owen screeched, rushing to put on his seatbelt and not relaxing until he heard the buckle click.

"Relax, I've driven so many times and I've only hit five curbs, three light posts, and two mailboxes." Jake insisted, relaxing his grip ever so slightly. "Besides, it's not like anyone's on the road." He added, pointing out that the usual rural traffic was nowhere to be found.

"I... I guess you're right." Owen reluctantly agreed after a moment of just listening to the engine hum.

"You're darn right I'm right." Jake boasted. "Ack! The turn!" He then quickly jerked the wheel to the right. Owen grabbed on to the ceiling handle and pulled his body close together, while Jake cackled as he took the sharp turn. The weight of the truck shifted drastically and it lifted up the passengers side as it turned.

"WHOOO!"

"OHH MAN!"

The truck shook as all four of its tires hit the road again. They both sat in silence for a moment. Owen's eyes were wide, his mouth hung open and his body trembled. He closed his mouth for a second, then opened it again.

"We could've *flipped* man!" Owen shrieked as he slowly unstuck himself from the small ball he was.

"But we didn't!" Jake pointed out with a laugh. "If I hadn't turned it hard we would've landed in the ditch." He explained.

"There are like, three ways to get down here." Owen explained in a slight snarl.

"But that way was more fun." Jake insisted while taking another turn, only more slow and carefully. "Admit it, it was fun."

Owen stayed quiet for a second, then slowly nodded and smiled. "Yeah, that was fun." He shook his head and rolled his eyes.

"That's the spirit." Jake took his hand off the wheel to elbow him.

"Don't miss this turn." Owen pointed to the small concrete driveway hidden by trees, leaves, and bushes.

"Got it!" Jake turned the steering wheel hard to the left and felt the small incline of the concrete meeting the road. Both of them bounced out of their chairs and fell back down.

Owen tried his best to catch his breath from laughing so hard. "Here we... are." His voice went from excited to brittle in a flash. His expression dropped, his mouth hanging open as he stared into the nothingness that was in front of them. Where his house once stood, now looked like it didn't even exist. The small driveway led to nothing. The grass looked untouched and the trees shadowed the empty lot. Despite the shock and fright this brought, the sun shone bright in the sky.

Jake opened his mouth and quietly asked. "Dude, are you sure this was-"

"Yeah." Owen mouthed, speechless.

Chapter 2

Jake watched Owen slump in the chair. He felt terrible, but he wasn't sure what he could do.

"I'm going to see what happened." Jake told Owen as he slowly exited the truck. He didn't answer, Owen just stared straight out the window.

Jake shut the truck door and started walking around. "Ok. I just need to find neighbors. Not too hard." He mumbled to himself to keep the uncharacteristic quiet from getting to him. He walked up onto a wooden porch and knocked on the door. "Hello? Anyone home?" He asked.

The door swung open. "Hello?" A little girl walked out and looked around.

"Sweetie, who's there?" A female voice, probably her mother, asked from inside the house.

"Hello, miss." Jake called inside, but got cut off.

"There's no one out here." The little girl ran back inside, the door slowly shutting behind her.

Jake blinked, staring at the door for a minute to gather his thoughts. "Little kids are weird. I should knock again." He knocked on the door again then stepped away from the door.

"I'll get it this time sweetie." A muffled voice said, then the supposed mother opened the door. "Hello?" She asked, turning her head from side to side.

"Hi. Miss? Hello?" Jake stood there and waved his hands in front of her face. The woman swatted at her face.

"You might as well come out." She shouted, walking out onto the porch. "This isn't funny."

Jake took a few steps back. "Uhh..." His mouth hung open, his eyes narrowing slightly. "I'm right here." He answered, raising an eyebrow.

The woman walked back inside in a huff.

"Weird." Jake shrugged and walked off the porch. "Next house I guess." He murmured .

He walked up onto the next porch and knocked on the door. Barking came from inside, followed by muffled screaming.

"Knock it off!" A man spat, then swung the door open and shut it behind him.

"Hello mister, I need help." Jake started to explain.

"Woah! What-?" He blurted suddenly.

Jake turned around to look and see what the person saw. He was met with nothing. "Mister, are you ok?" He turned back around to face the man.

"No more drinks today." He said under his breath, looking very freaked out as he walked back inside.

"What is going on!?" Jake exclaimed, feeling like he was losing his mind. He walked onto the pavement and cupped his hands around his mouth. "HELLO?!" His voice echoed off the trees, making the silence that followed deafening.

"What are we supposed to do if the world's broken?" He asked under his breath. He was walking down Owen's driveway to the truck when he heard leaves rustling beside him.

"What's there?" Jake asked, jumping into a karate pose. He walked closer to the sound, but didn't lower his guard.

"Jake." Someone whispered in his ear and grabbed his shoulder.

"GAH!" He whipped around.

"Shhhh. Relax dude, it's me." Owen hushed Jake and took a step back. "I just saw the most freaky thing."

"Can't be more freaky than what happened to me." Jake mumbled.

"No, seriously. Trust me." Owen insisted, then signaled Jake to follow him. He followed behind him, watching Owen's body tremble as they crouched and walked closer to the truck.

"Look." Owen mumbled, pointing at a small field.

A cat was stalking a squirrel. When the cat leapt, it paused midway in the air and appeared back where it started. The squirrel stayed still beside the occasional twitch of its tail.

"Woah." He breathed, sending a tingle down his spine.

"What does this mean?" Owen matched his tone.

"I don't know." Jake replied, standing up straight. "Let's go back to the truck and talk."

They both walked back and got in their respective seats.

"You'll never guess what happened to me dude, it was so weird and scary." Jake started.

Owen's eyes widened and he squirmed in his seat.

"Dude? What's going on?" Jake asked, looking out where Owen was staring.

Owen pointed with his shaking arm, trying to

13

form words. "I- Wha- I-I- Dude- Look!" He stuttered.

"What dude? You're freaking me out!" Jake exclaimed. He saw nothing, but he felt an overwhelming sense of danger.

"Drive dude drive!" Owen screeched, buckling quickly.

Jake grabbed his seat belt and slid it on before grasping the steering wheel and gear shift. He threw it in reverse and sped out of there like his life depended on it, which it kind of did.

"What did you see dude?" Jake questioned as he drove to an unknown destination.

Owen sat there, stunned and almost hyperventilating.

"Look, we're far away from whatever it was. Just tell me." Jake pushed, but didn't take his eyes off the road.

Owen tried to catch his breath, sighing every once in a while. "I don't know what I saw, man. I just... I heard a faint voice that said to run, then the thing growled. I-I seriously don't know dude." His voice wavered as he spoke, still shaken.

"So you're hearing things now?" Jake summed up what he heard.

"I-I guess?" Owen covered his face with his hands.

"Look, it's getting..." Jake paused. "Dark? Maybe? What time even is it?" He mumbled. "It's been crazy. You need to sleep off the adrenaline." He explained. "Go lay down in the back and I'll wake you up if anything happens."

"I don't know. What if something happens and you-"

"I'll figure it out." Jake cut him off.

"Ok." Owen mumbled and slowly slid into the

backseat.

Jake drove in silence for a while, throwing thoughts back and forth, but nothing really stuck. What's going on and where are all the normal people? The sun slowly started to set, at least he thought that's what was happening. He wasn't really sure what was happening anymore. The crazy weather, the weird thing that happened at school, the people ignoring him, the cat and mouse, that monster. He wanted to figure it out but there is no real way of doing that.

"Is the sun really setting or is it just going to stay at blinding level forever?" He asked himself under his breath. He squinted his eyes and tried to find out where he was. "No signs? Really?" He muttered. "Better than anything else I guess."

Sometimes he'd hear random echoes of honking that scared him half to death, but other than that it seems like a normal day. Jake yawned, feeling his eyes getting heavier each minute.

"I'll have to pull over soon, but thanks to scardy-cat in the back seat, I don't know if it's safe to stop anymore." He murmured to the nothingness. Jake pointed the air conditioning at his face to help him stay awake. It helped, but after a while his eyes started to sting and water.

"Nope, that's it. I'm pulling over." He sighed. "This is a hotel place thing right?" He pulled into an Inn's parking lot and parked the car. He hopped out, looking around for an open room. Jake jiggled three door handles until he felt one open.

"Jackpot." He pumped his fist and walked into the room. The room was small, with one bed and bathroom, but it would work for both of them. He walked back to the car to see Owen groggily crawling out from the back seat.

"Good. Passenger princess's awake." Jake noted when he opened Owens door.

"Dude…" He grumbled, narrowing his eyes at the nickname. "Why did we stop?"

"I'm getting tired, so I found this place." Jake explained while helping Owen slide out of the car.

Owen shrugged. "Ok." Both walked over to the room Jake found before Owen paused. "Did you pay for this room?"

"Pay?"

"Dude."

Jake groaned. "Do you think, after *everything* that's happened, *paying* is the thing to be worried about?"

"Fine." Owen gave in and they both walked into the room.

Jake shut the door behind them and flicked the lights back on. "This was the first one I found." He explained before joining Owen on the bed.

"So we just hope and pray that everything goes back to normal in the morning." Owen sighed and actually looked relaxed for the first time that day. He inched his way up to the headboard and leaned against it.

"I don't see anything else we could do." Jake agreed, climbing beside him. He folded his arms behind his head.

"Do you have your phone?" Owen asked while continuously switching channels with the remote, all of them showing up with static and streaks of neon.

"I think so." Jake reached into his pocket and handed it to Owen.

Owen turned the tv off and turned on Jake's phone. "No date. No time." He murmured. "Just weird symbols." Owen showed Jake his phone. It looked like a mix of a two-year-olds writing and a different language.

Jake's lip curled slightly in confusion. "Why does the time and date matter anymore?" He asked, leaning forward to cover his face with his hands. "This whole world is falling apart." He yawned and rubbed his face with his palms.

"Go to sleep dude." Owen placed a hand on the back of his head. "I'll go look and see if there's food anywhere around here."

"Alright, you go do that." Jake mumbled while slowly sliding under the covers. He yawned again and closed his eyes.

-_-_-_-_-_-

Jake's body was heavy when he woke up. He wasn't sure what day it was and how much time passed, but he didn't feel all that rested. His mind didn't feel ready to process anything yet, so he turned his head into the pillow and inched his way under the covers. Suddenly, something thrashed him around and knocked him out of the bed.

"Oh-...well that works I guess." Owen said while peering over the side of the bed.

"Duuude..." Jake groaned, not moving from the floor and feeling like a weighted puddle under the blanket.

"Wake up dude."

"Why?" Jake muttered, pulling the blanket away from his face without moving his arms.

"Because I found food."

"Ooo, ok." Jake dragged himself off the floor using the bed and his love for food.

"We have to cook up a few of the things though." Owen warned.

"Don't worry dude, I've been cooking since I was like five." Jake ensured as he sat on the bed and looked through all the boxed and canned items Owen found.

"Really?" Owen asked, tilting his head slightly.

"Not since five, but yeah." Jake shrugged, opening up a small bag of chips. "Good thinking with the boxes and cans." He said while chewing.

"That's all I could find." Owen explained while picking through the items.

Both of them sat in silence as they ate. Jake occasionally looked out of the window and observed how cloudy it kept getting.

"Do you think it will rain?" Jake asked, breaking the silence.

Owen shrugged. "Maybe." He went back to eating his small container of cereal.

"When you were in the truck yesterday, you'll never guess what happened."

"What?" Owen's voice muffled through the cereal.

Jake explained what happened when he tried to find help. "But when I looked to see what the noise was, you came and found me."

"Yeah, I heard you scream." Owen admitted. "I kind of thought about screaming back." He snickered.

"Ha ha. Very funny." Jake sighed.

"It would have been." Owen elbowed him in the side. "About that creature thing, what happens if we see it again?" He took a bite of cereal.

Jake shrugged. "I'll throw you at it as a distraction."

Owen's eyes widened and he quickly swallowed.

"Dude I'm joking." Jake stated quickly before

18

taking a bite of his chips. He swallowed before starting to talk again. "I don't know, I guess we'd just run away like last time. Why?"

"It's just in the back of my mind." Owen shrugged.

"Did you see anything weird at the store?" Jake asked.

"No, not really." Owen looked down at his cereal. Keys jingled from outside, making them turn their heads. It went silent for a moment as Jake placed his bag on the bed. He slowly slid off and tiptoed to the door. He pressed his ear against the cold door.

"Here's my room." A man's muffled voice said over and over along with keys jingling. Jake crawled over to the window beside the door and slid the curtain slightly to peek out.

The man stood there, continuously stating "Here's my room." while moving the keys up to the keyhole and back down to his side. It seemed like he was a broken npc in a video game.

"What's out there?" Owen asked quietly.

"Just a man, but he's blocking the door completely." Jake explained.

"Then how do we get out? Do we just crawl out the window?" Owen questioned.

"I don't think we have to leave." Jake sat down on the bed. "As long as he doesn't come in we should be fine." He said before picking his chips back up and starting to eat again. They both sat on the bed, listening to the man. At one point Jake thought he heard the guy say "Here they are", but thought he was just going crazy.

"I'm going to look." Owen murmured as he got off the bed.

"Ok." Jake watched him crawl over to the window

and push the curtain back. Owen peered out before jumping back and shuffling his back into the side of the bed.

Jake quickly stood up, looking down at Owen. "Dude, what is-" He looked up at the window and his eyes met a yellow-green predatory eye staring through the crack of the window. "Dude?" He mumbled as his eyes slowly slid down to look at Owen again.

Air escaped Owen's open mouth as he tried to form words. Jake looked back up at the monster as it snarled.

Chapter 3

The monster glared into the room but didn't make any move to get in. Saliva dripped from its sharp teeth and large mouth.

"How do we get out of here?" Jake mumbled to Owen. Owen's mouth was dry and his head hurt as one thought kept screaming in his mind, the window. But how the window?

Engine noises revved from outside, quickly coming closer until it slammed into the monster. It roared, the sound feeling like a loud bass at a concert.

"Come on dude, let's go!" Jake grabbed Owen's wrist and started to pull him up off the ground.

"Let's go out the window." Owen grabbed Jake's arm and helped pull himself the rest of the way.

"Ok." Jake let go of Owen's wrist and went to open the window. Owen followed behind Jake as they climbed out the window and landed onto the soaked concrete. They both looked over at the monster and saw a large cement truck slam into it, knocking it to the ground and giving them time to run behind the building.

"What are we going to do?" Jake panted and placed his hands on his knees.

Owen leaned his body against the building as he tried to catch his breath. "What... do you mean?"

"The trucks up there. We can't leave without it."

"Yes you can."

Both of them stood up straight and turned to address the voice. Owen's wobbly legs struggled to hold up his weight as he took a step toward the man. The only thing Owen could take in was that the man looked tall and thin.

"Who- who are you?" Owen asked as Jake came to stand beside him.

"I'm Theo. But that doesn't matter right now. We'll have time for introductions later. Right now, we have to get out of here while it's distracted."

"But how?" Jake asked.

"Don't worry about that, we have a plan." Theo explained as the monster let out a loud yelp, making all of them jump slightly. "Stay right here." He tapped the brick wall. Owen leaned against the wall again and the man walked back to the front of the building.

"We?" Owen mumbled to Jake.

Jake shrugged. "Maybe the guy in that truck." He suggested.

"Yeah, maybe." Owen mumbled, looking over at the supermarket across the sidewalk. He thought the person sounded familiar, but it was obvious that they hadn't seen each other before. It was probably the adrenaline from what was going on. That's what was happening. He assured himself.

"Are we going to listen to him?" Jake asked, breaking the silence. "It's not like we really have a choice."

"But they're probably..." Owen started as Jake came and leaned against the wall beside him. "These guys are probably..."

"...Probably?" Jake repeated.

"I... I don't know. The broken people?" Owen hesitated. "Like the guy knocking at the door."

"Yeah, maybe." Jake nodded. "But come on man. He talked to us." He waved his hand between him and Owen a few times. "That's a lot more than I got from the other people."

"True." Owen mumbled. "We can let them help us, but we can't put down our guard." He said a little louder.

"Alright, there's a plan." Jake folded his arms. "Now we need a name for the broken people."

"Ok, you come up with that." Owen looked down at his shoes, listening to Jake spout out names every few seconds.

"Are you boys still back here?" The man came running around the corner, startling them both.

"Yes sir." Jake said enthusiastically as he jumped off the wall. Owen slowly followed behind him.

"Good." Theo placed a hand on Jake's shoulder. "Come with me, we've got something to explain but we can't do it here."

"Something to explain?" Owen questioned.

"Why not here?" Jake asked, cutting Owen off.

"Yes, something to explain in the truck." He answered Owen. "Not here because the monster could get back up in any moment." The loud sound of the cement truck increased as it rolled around the corner. The man looked up from them both, taking his hand off Jake.

"Are they coming, Theo?" The man in the truck shouted out the rolled window to Theo while stopping it beside them. They all stared at him.

"Look." Theo turned back to look at them,

competing with the noisy truck. " I know there's no reason to trust us, but if you stay here that thing in the front will get a hold of you." He paused to let them think about it.

Jake turned to Owen. "What do you think dude?" He asked. "I think we should go."

Owen hesitated. "Me too... but-."

"I know." Jake took a step toward Owen and whispered. "But look at our other options." The truck. Their truck in the front is the only other option, other than running. But the front is where the monster is, and they'd probably break their ankles after the first mile if they ran.

Owen sighed. "Ok. Let's go."

"WHOO! Road trip!" Jake threw his fist into the air as he turned around. Both of them followed Theo to the passenger side. He opened the door and Jake jumped right in beside the other man.

"Hello boys, I'm Jack." The man behind the wheel greeted them as they climbed in.

"Hi. I'm Jake, and this is Owen." Jake introduced them both as he slid across the bench seat and buckled himself in. Owen followed Jake down the gray leather seats and pulled the buckle across his chest.

"Nice to meet you both." Jack dipped his head to them as Theo got in and closed the door. "And don't worry about being so squished, this truck's only temporary." He patted the wheel and started driving. It dragged for a few seconds until they got to the road, then it only took a second for it to take off. Owen felt the cold air from outside smack his face, but it felt nice. It let him know that he was still alive or at least awake.

"Have any of you boys ever rode in a cement truck

before?" Jack asked, letting his elbow hang out the open window.

"I tried to sneak into one if that counts." Jake said nonchalantly.

"Why would you need to sneak into one?" Jack asked, followed by Theo asking concerned.

"Why would you sneak into one in the first place? It's illegal to sneak into someone else's property, let alone dangerous." The last part sounded more directed to Jack than to Jake.

Owen let their voices flow through one ear and out the other. He looked over at Jake and Jack. Jake looked like an exact copy of Jack, well not exact. Jack looked like he could lift the cement truck and work for construction, while Jake could pass as a younger version of him, or Jack's son. Even their names were similar. Owen looked out at the road in front of them, letting his mind wander. This place is getting too weird and scary, and he wasn't sure how long his mind could keep up with it.

"How long until you think we can switch vehicles?" Theo asked, catching Owen's attention.

"Until we find one." Jack sighed through his teeth. "Why? Do you think now's a good time?"

Theo turned to look out of the window beside him. "I didn't say anything about that."

"About what?" Jake asked, turning to look at Theo who kept staring at the window. Jake practically read Owen's mind.

Theo slowly turned to face him. "It's none of your business right now, ok?" He put his arm behind Owen and placed a hand on Jake's shoulder. "We'll tell you when we're further away, but for right now just trust that we have your best interest at heart."

Owen felt lightheaded when Theo spoke. Why did Jack get so upset? Theo didn't say anything upsetting, at least he thought. What did he mean by that, and what did he know about their best interests? What even were their best interests?

"Soooo... do you guys know each other?" Jake asked, probably sensing the tension and trying to break it.

"Yeah. We've been friends since college." Jack started explaining.

"We went to the same high school, but we... weren't that close back then." Theo added, letting the silence bubble around them. They stayed like that for a few minutes, watching trees, strip malls, and houses fly past them. After the long awkward silence, they finally found a car dealership filled with several types of vehicles. Jack pulled in and parked in one of the empty spaces next to a row of minivans.

"Alright, let's find one and hop in." Jack flung his door open and the cement truck engine stopped. "Well, that's new." He mumbled, not bothering to take the keys with them.

"I think you'll like this sir." An uptight sounding voice inched toward them, though there wasn't a person with it. All of them tumbled out of the truck and walked around as they tried to identify where the voice were coming from.

"Wow, freaky." Jake said, followed by a quiet shush from Theo.

"This ain't the time to talk, boy." Jack leaded down and muttered to Jake. He then stepped in front of them all and blocked the wind with his large body. He stopped and surveyed the area, stopping them with an outstretched arm. "This way." He mouthed, waving his arm away from the voice. They all tiptoed behind him, in front of the vehicles and toward the building.

"I thought you said this wasn't the time to talk." Jake teased, earning a scoff from Jack.

"We're further away now, so they can't hear us." Jack explained quietly.

"Do you think you can tell us now?" Jake whispered, looking up at Jack.

"About what? The thing we were talking about in the car?" Jack sighed, walking three feet before answering. "I guess, but once we get inside, I don't know who or what is out here. But whatever it is, I bet it ain't nothing good." The silence hung until they reached the large glass doors and display windows. Jack opened the door and waved them all inside. As they made their way inside, they adjusted to the dark building.

"So, we're looking for keys?" Theo asked once Jack shut the door.

Jack nodded. "But I suggest we all stay together."

"Agreed." Theo nodded, his voice sounding quiet in the large room. Jack and Theo walked ahead of Jake and Owen behind a few desks.

"Are you going to tell us now?" Jake asked, and Owen gave a small "Yeah" in agreement.

Theo sighed, his shoulders drooping for a moment before turning to look at Jack and asked. "Once we get another car we'll explain?"

"No!" Jake blurted, stopping in his tracks. Owen took a step back. Everyone stopped walking to turn and look at Jake. "You're telling us now. No more excuses."

"This ain't a way to talk to an adult, boy." Jack replied.

"Look, if you won't tell us we'll leave." Jake argued. "We've made it this far haven't we?" Owen's mouth opened and his eyes widened at Jake's statement. His mind started spiraling into chaos. No! No they haven't! He's trying to get us killed! Owen stayed silent while Theo tried to keep everyone calm.

"All because we found and saved you boy!" Jack spat.

"Everyone! Let's try to keep our heads." Theo pleaded. He then turned to Jack and muttered into his ear through gritted teeth. "If you don't tell them right now, I'll leave you here alone and I'll tell them."

"Fine." Jack grumbled. "We'll tell you."

Owen sighed, his body relaxing. It must be something crazy if they keep trying to put it off.

"Let's keep walking, we've wasted too much time just standing here." Jack started to walk off quickly, leaving them all to catch up with him.

After following behind Jack in silence, Owen grabbed his fleeting courage. "So... what is it?" He murmured to Theo.

Theo placed a hand on Owen's back. "We should probably sit down for this. It will break your whole understanding."

Jack sighed. "I'll find keys then." He stomped off.

They all stopped walking and grabbed chairs from nearby desks. Theo sat in front of Jake and Owen, who sat close together.

"I'm pretty sure you boys know that what is going on is not normal in the slightest." Theo started and both of them stayed silent, nodding slowly. Theo sighed, placing his head into his hands as he leaned forward. "Look, there isn't a way to sugarcoat this at all. So I'm just going to say it." Both of them nodded. Owen gripped the armrests with anxious anticipation.

Theo hesitated for a second before looking up and talking. "That monster... this- this whole place. It isn't real." They both stayed silent, so he continued. "We came here to save you both. We're not a part of this whole mess, I promise." He paused again, but after being met with silence once more he continued. "That monster is after you Owen. That's why we have to keep moving."

Somehow the revelation wasn't shocking Owen as much as he thought it would. He already put together that the monster was after them, so that didn't scare him as much as the first part.

"So... we're the only..." Jake quietly trailed off. He took a deep breath before starting over. "We're the only real people."

Theo paused, letting out a breath. "Jack and I are real too."

"What about our parents?" Owen asked in a quiet voice, that somehow made the building even quieter.

Theo reached forward and placed his hands on Owen's. "That is what I was dreading to talk about the most." He hung his head for what felt like forever. When he met Owen's eyes again, they were filled with tears. "I'm... I'm your father."

Owen let that sink in, his tears making the light coming from outside look blurry. Theo slid out of the chair and reached his arms around Owen.

"I never wanted you in here son, and I hope you believe me. I'm here to fight and protect you like I should have." Theo's voice started to break. Jake reached over and wrapped his arms around Theo and Owen.

They sat like that for what felt like ages. Owen

took a shaky breath in and out. "What about Jake?" He asked, his voice muffled by Theo's chest.

"What do you mean?" Theo asked, his voice strained by quiet tears.

"What about his family?"

Theo let out a shaky breath. "Him and Jack are related." He explained softly.

Jack rounded the corner, sounding much calmer now. "So, you told them." He walked over, knelt down, and placed an arm around Jake.

"Yes, I did. I think they'll be more willing to come with us now." Theo explained to Jack.

"Then let's roll out." Jack stood up. "The monster will come after us sooner than later."

Chapter 4

A two door truck beeped and flashed its lights a few car spaces away from the entrance of the car dealership.

"Well, would you look at that?" Jack walked toward the truck, everyone following him. "Let's get in and head out."

Owen was breathing down Jake's neck as they moved across the dead silent parking lot. The cold wind hit them in all directions and Jake looked up at the sky. The gray storm clouds slid across the sky toward them.

"Does it look like it's going to rain to you?" Jake whispered into Owen's ear, trying to keep up with Theo and Jack as he leaned his head back.

Owen nodded. "Maybe we should stay here until it passes?" He added quietly.

Jake took two big steps, reached up, and tapped Theo's shoulder. "We think it would be best to stay here until these clouds pass."

Theo looked up, seeing the clouds reach and cover the sun. "I don't think that would be a bad idea. What do you think Jack?"

"I think we should get going." Jack unlocked the truck. "I bet that monster will be here any moment.

And this tiny thing won't take that big of a beating." He explained, walking to the driver's side door after tapping the hood twice.

"Alright." Theo sighed.

When they all got in the truck, the clouds had taken over the sky and bouncy ball sized hail started being pelted at the truck. Jack started up the truck but smacked the steering wheel then he saw rain falling from the sky. It slowly started covering everything it touched in ice.

"You can't be serious!" He spat. "Freezing rain?!" He sighed, placing his head on the steering wheel. They all sat there in awkward silence until Jack spoke again, sounding more calm. "I'll drive it under the doors canopy so we can all get out and hopefully have an intact truck." He grumbly explained. He slowly drove under the canopy and helped everyone out. Jake thought about catching one of the balls of hail but decided against it. They all walked back inside and sat in the chairs they left. Jack pulled up a chair beside Theo and whispered something to him. Theo shrugged and whispered something back.

"I'm going to see if there's any food in here." Jack spoke to the group before standing up and walking away.

"Why is he so angry?" Jake asked Theo once Jack went down a small hall.

"He has a set plan in his mind, and we've completely strayed off the path." Theo explained. "He's not like this always." He sighed. "Jack just has to give up the fact that what happens now is out of his control."

Jake slumped in his chair, looking out the window. It was cloudy and he was almost unable to even see the cars in the parking lot, yet light flooded the building and seemed to reach every crevice and corner. "Do you think the monster will find us through all of that?" Jake wondered out loud, turning to Owen.

Owen shrugged. "Maybe."

"I would guess so." Theo added. "This whole thing might be rigged against us." He pushed himself out of the chair. "I'd suggest finding anything that may help us in the long run. First aid, clothing, water." He listed. "I'd rather have it and not need it, than need it and not have it. But you both are free to do whatever you want." Theo walked over to Owen and placed a hand on his shoulder. "Be safe son." He then let go and walked down the same hallway Jack went into.

"So, do we want to go search for stuff?" Jake asked after a few minutes of sitting in silence. He looked over at Owen, who stared back at him with a somewhat blank stare.

"I don't know man." Owen shrugged. "What do you think this place is if it isn't real?" He asked.

Jake sighed. "I don't know dude. Maybe we're in an alternate reality or something. OOH! Or!" He enthusiastically sat up in his seat. "Maybe we're in something like the matrix!"

Owen stared at him, looking confused yet entirely done with him.

"Think about it dude. We could do those crazy flips and all that. That would be cool."

"I don't think we're on a machine ship." Owen mumbled, turning to face the window.

"What's on your mind dude?" Jake asked, finally getting around to see why he was so quiet.

Owen slumped forward in the chair. "I didn't tell you before, but in the motel I heard that voice again." He started quietly. Jake slumped forward to look Owen in the eye. "I think... I think Theo's the voice." He turned his head at Jake.

Jake blinked, unsure what to do with that information. "And that means?"

"That means that we can probably rule out being in the matrix." Owen explained. "But that opens the question of how he was able to do that."

"I wouldn't worry about it." Jake sat up in his chair. "The only thing I'd worry about is the storm." Hail the size of apples were beating against the large windows.

"Maybe we should find Theo and Jack." Owen proposed.

Jake watched the hail hit the window, over and over again. It looked like in any second the glass would break. "Yeah, let's do that."

They both stood up and walked down the hall Jack and Theo went down. Jake kept thinking about what the place could be. It could be something close to the matrix maybe? It was strange he didn't tell us what this place was. If they were on our side...

Jake grabbed Owen's arm and pulled him back from one of the doors before he went in.

"Dude, what-"

"I feel like they're keeping something from us." Jake explained after flattening himself against the wall.

"And you just thought of that now?" Owen asked, sounding sceptical.

"I just think it's weird that we don't know what this place is?"

Owen stared at Jake and folded his arms. "I'm guessing you don't mean the dealership." He mumbled.

"If we are in something like the matrix, wouldn't it be good to know?" Jake asked Owen, giving it a second to sink in. "Also, I bet they know a way out and that's why they're so eager to get back on the road."

"It makes sense." Owen agreed. "But they're grown-ups. And Theo's..." His thought trailed off, and Jake didn't have to hear the next word to know what he was saying.

"Yes but- the monster... is that our only threat?" Jake paused, not wanting to think about the thing he was about to say. "Or is there something bigger and more dangerous out there about to come out of the sky and eat us!"

Owen's eyes widened and he shrank back slightly. "I-I don't want to know dude." He shook his head like, probably clearing the image that Jake wished he could. "But if that is something to worry about..." He sighed. "I guess I'd want to know before it happened."

"I'm not trying to suggest they're trying to lead us to danger." Jake quickly added. He didn't want to make Owen think his father was a bad guy. If anything, he thought Jack might be despite supposedly being related to him. "I'm just... suggesting we continue to keep our guard up."

"Maybe find supplies just for ourselves just in case?" Owen suggested.

"Exactly." Jake nodded. "Now, let's keep trying to find Jack and Theo."

Both of them continued walking, checking every doorway and hallway until hearing Jack call to them.

"Hey boys, is that you?" He walked out into the hallway and sighed. "Phew." He wiped his forehead of invisible sweat. "I'm glad you guys decided to help. I think I found an employee lounge." He led them into a large, well-lit room with multiple tables, chairs, and even two couches. Jake felt it kind of out of place, but he wasn't going to complain if this helped them. "Grab food, paper towels, anything that you think would be useful."

"What about soap?" Owen asked, picking up a small dispenser of hand soap off a counter near a sink.

"We can use that." Jack nodded. "I'm going to find Theo, you all stay here."

"He didn't find you?" Jake asked, concern slowly slipping into his thoughts. Out of the corner of his eye, he saw Owen look up from a cabinet he was looking through.

"He found me. We found a bathroom and decided to split up." Jack explained. "I told him I'd go find him after I saw if you boys were ok. I'm just going to tell him now." He assured the boys before stepping out of the room and walking down the hallway.

Owen let out an audible sigh of relief.

"I feel ya." Jake started looking in the cabinets above where Owen was checking out. "Whatcha find so far?" He asked, pulling down plastic cups.

"Cleaning supplies." Owen answered, pulling out several rolls of paper towels and unused soap dispensers.

"I wonder if they found bags yet."

"Maybe." Owen shrugged, pulling himself up with the counter. "Ooo, donuts!" He opened the box and found crumbs. "Awe. They ate them all."

"Digital scums." Jake laughed as Owen threw the box away. "Yo, what if we're digital?"

"That would be kind of weird don't you think?" But Owen shrugged. "But I guess that's a possibility too."

"I'm checking that closet." Jake pointed to a door before walking over to check it out.

"Alright." Owen turned around to check more cabinets.

Jake opened the door and gasped. Food! Lots of food. Enough for them for two seconds Jake thought. "Dude check this out." He called over to Owen, who quickly made his way over.

"Wow. That's a lot of boxes of chips. They must eat a lot." Owen noted.

"What did you boys find?" Jack asked, startling them both.

"Looks like enough food to feed... well, I guess the people who work here." Theo placed his hand on Owen's shoulder as he walked past them into the closet. "We should take this to the front so we don't have to come back for it later."

They all agreed, everyone picking up as many boxes as they could and slowly followed Jack to the front. Jake swore it was getting colder the more they walked, but he shook the thought away when he almost tripped over Owen, who almost tripped over Theo, who almost tripped over Jack. As they walked, they talked about what they found.

"The bathroom closet had soap, paper towels, three first aid kits, and toilet paper." Theo started explaining to them before being cut off by the sound of glass shattering and thick gusts of wind blowing over everyone's boxes.

"You two get in the back, we'll check this out." Jack turned his head while blocking the hallway with his body.

Jake and Owen ran, not hesitating to see if it was the monster. Knowing their luck, it was. They didn't stop before hitting two double doors, leading to an office. Both of them tried to catch their breath before throwing the doors open. Jake and Owen ran in and slammed their bodies on the door.

"We need something to block the door." Jake motioned for Owen to stay holding the door while he positioned his back up against the desk. He pushed with his legs with scary effort, but it didn't budge. "Owen. It won't budge, come help." Owen raced over, matching Jake's stance and together, they made it move an inch.

Owen pointed to large filing cabinets. "What about those?" He asked, between breaths. Jake nodded, getting on one side of the metal cabinet and waited for Owen to get on the other side. They pushed it off the wall with their hands, it felt close to the weight of the desk but somehow it was lighter. They pushed it to the door, flinching backward when it almost fell over.

Jake let out a quick deep breath. "Two more?" Owen nodded. They repeated what they did with the first one, placing them in front of the tinted windows set in the doors.

They both flopped to the floor, panting as they used the cabinets to sit up. "What now?" Owen murmured.

"I guess we wait." Jake replied under his breath. "Maybe we should hide under the desk?" Both of them crawled over to behind the desk, then shuffled their backs into the hole meant for a large chair and the person's legs. Their breathing sounded amplified in the small space. "This is a twisted game of hide and seek." Jake joked.

Owen didn't laugh. "Yeah, really."

"Dude, they'll be fine." Jake tried to reassure Owen. "I bet it isn't even the monster. It's probably just a bunch of hail." He explained. "In fact, I bet they're looking for us now to explain the whole situation."

It looked like Owen was staring at the dark wood behind Jake when he nodded. His gaze felt distant and Jake looked at him. Jake bet they were both starting to feel tired, they were just carrying boxes, then ran for what felt like three straight minutes, tried to move this heavy desk but switched to less heavy filing cabinets, then cramped themselves underneath the large desk. His stomach twisted and his lungs felt empty despite him obviously breathing. Jake was trying to make himself believe that they were fine, but with the storm still crashing into the side of the building and the monster possibly being there... it made him feel helpless without knowing anything.

Chapter 5

Owen leaned his head against the desk, his body feeling like it was just run over and being crushed by a semi truck. He wanted everything to be ok. He wanted everything to go back to normal. Owen tried to listen to what was happening, but it was quiet which made him even more anxious. He couldn't help but think that they were hurt, or even worse, dead. He closed his eyes and squashed himself into an even smaller ball.

"Should we check and see if it's ok to come out?" Jake asked quietly, leaning closer to Owen. He opened his eyes and looked at Jake. He looked so calm somehow, yet he was hunched over and looked ready to jump out.

Owen took a deep breath and shrugged. "Maybe?"

A loud slam from the door made them shuffle closer together. Owen's body started to tremble and shut off, his body freezing up.

"Boys, are you in there!?" Jack's concerned muffled scream came from the other side of the door.

Both of them let out an audible sigh of relief and slowly climbed out from under the desk. "Yeah, we're in here!" Jake shouted to Jack once he got to his feet. Owen sluggishly slid his way out and leaned his body on the desk when he finally got to his feet. His body felt ridiculously sore as he listened for Jack's reply.

"What did you put in front of the door? It feels like cement blocks!"

"It's filing cabinets!" Jake answered, pressing his body as close to the door as the filing cabinets allowed.

"Can you move them?" Jack asked. Jake waved Owen over and the both tried to move the one in front of the door handles. They grunted and Owen's face scrunched together as he tried to pull his side. Jake stopped pulling after moving it an inch. Owen lost his grip and fell onto his back.

"Ow." Owen scoffed and Jake came over to help him stand.

"Are you ok dude?"

"Yeah, I'm good." Owen rubbed his lower back. "Man did that hurt." He said quietly under his breath while Jake responded.

"No, we can't!"

A loud sigh came from the other side of the door. "Get away from the door!" Jack shouted, leaving them a short time to walk to the side before a slam came from the door. The filing cabinets wobbled but inched forward. A second slam caused the middle cabinet to fall onto the desk and break it in half. "Are you boys ok!?" Jack called to them before pushing one door.

"Yeah, we're fine." Jake responded. "This desk isn't though."

Jack slid the filing cabinet along with the door and walked over to them. He leaned his body on the wall, his shoulder slumping. "It was just the hail breaking the glass." He explained, somehow looking older as he pushed himself up off the wall. "Come on. We can't stay

41

here now that the glass is broken."

"Where's Theo?" Owen quietly managed to ask.

"He's trying to find bags up front." Jack started explaining as they walked over to the door and down the hallway. I'm thinking the only thing we'll find is something small with the dealership's logo on it. But I'm sure we can carry most of the things we found. We'll just have to be... creative."

"So where are we going now?" Jake asked.

"I think I saw a store across the road when we got here, I'm going to head over there and see what I can find." Jack yawned. "We'll probably find somewhere to lay low for the night."

Owen couldn't believe it was night already, it didn't feel like they were here that long. But this place was doing crazy things to their mind. It wouldn't seem that out of character for it to be messing with their sense of time. "Alright." Owen mumbled, nodding.

"Will you take someone to the store with you?" Jake walked past Jack and threw up his hand like answering a question. He stopped and faced Jake. "I volunteer to go."

Jack stopped in front of Jake and sighed. "We'll either all go... or I'll go." He got closer to whisper something in his ear that Owen didn't catch. That made him worry a bit, but Jake didn't protest.

"I understand." Jake turned and they all kept walking. The hallway seemed to stretch on and on, and the silence didn't make it better. Warped pictures of CEO's and employee's of the month appeared on the wall every once in a while. Some flickered in and out while others looked vaguely inhuman which freaked him out a bit.

"You boys did a great job barricading the door." Jack praised while placing his hand on his shoulder. "I'm gonna be sore tomorrow."

"We were going for the desk at first, but we couldn't move it." Jake explained. "So we went for the cabinets instead."

"I'm surprised that you could move them at all." Jack sounded like he was in shock and awe at the fact two teenage boys with an adrenaline boost could move three tall, metal filing cabinets. In Jack's defense, Owen was shocked they could move them too.

They walked the rest of the way up in silence, listening to the sound of hail getting louder as they got closer. Something Owen noticed while walking, looking into some of the rooms, some of them were pitch black and empty. It didn't make much sense, seeing that other rooms and the hallway, the lights were on. They walked out of the hallway and were out in the front again. Rain, hail, and ice were making the large hole in the glass bigger by the second. It made the room freezing despite only being the beginning of fall.

"It's freezing in here." Jake said what Owen was thinking.

"Yeah, so we better be quick." Jack stated. "You two start opening boxes and stuffing stuff inside."

"The chip boxes?" Jake walked over to the yellow boxes stacked on the side of the wall. "Do you want us to try and fit most of the chips into a few boxes and use the empty ones for other things?" He asked.

"That works." Jack nodded. "I'm going to find Theo. He's up here somewhere." He walked off and left Jake and Owen to their task.

They started opening boxes, Jake dumped chips out onto the floor and Owen shoved chips into his open boxes. They paused, looking over at the hallway and looking at the lights. They flickered on and off, sort of like strobe lights but much more ominous, like something from a scary movie.

"The sooner we finish this, the sooner we're out of here." Jake reminded Owen and they both quickly returned to the task at hand. Owen pushed the flickering lights to the back of his mind and kept them there as he continued shoving chips into boxes.

"I think that's it for chips." Owen informed Jake before shuffling over to the other side on his knees.

"Let's start packing the other supplies in then." Jake grabbed paper towels and started placing them inside the empty boxes.

"I suggest you boys pack two of everything into a few boxes. We need all of this stuff, not just a bunch of paper towels." Theo told them before dropping to his knees to help. Jack got down on his knees too, and started handing things to Owen.

"I'm guessing you didn't find any bags?" Jake asked, stuffing two toilet paper rolls into a box.

"No." Theo shook his head, handing Owen two water bottles. "I didn't find anything else either. My hope is that we'll be able to find some over at that store, if it exists."

"It should exist." Jack countered. "I just hope we won't have to go over there by foot." He added.

"Are you afraid of being spotted by people?" Theo asked. "I don't think that should be our main concern."

"I didn't say that." Jack passed Jake a first aid kit. "I'm just saying that we still have to watch for cars. And I haven't been able to see any on the road for some reason."

"We ran into that problem too." Jake started to reply.

"We did?" Owen cut him off.

"Yeah, but you were asleep." Jake answered before addressing Jack again. "It didn't seem to be a problem. I didn't run into anyone at least. I did hear honking though."

Jack seemed to be soaking in the information as he handed Jake a few items. "Alright. We'll just have to be careful."

"Do you think using a car will be dangerous?" Theo asked, looking over at the full boxes before standing up.

Jack sighed and nodded. "I just don't see any other choices other than going on foot." He shrugged, also standing.

"I think that's all we can pack up boys." Theo told them before reaching down a hand to help Owen up. Owen grabbed his hand and got up off the ground, though his body protested. It wanted to stay and lay there forever but he forced himself up anyway.

"Alright boys, let's grab a few boxes and start heading out." Jack pointed to the boxes and grabbed five. Jake grabbed four, and Theo and Owen grabbed three before they walked over to the doors. "Can someone open that?"

Owen nodded and walked in front of everyone to push the door open with his back. The freezing rain had turned to snow and the hail shrank down to the size of marbles, making the overall situation a little easier. That still didn't mean the hail hurt any less or it didn't feel any colder.

"It's freezing out here." Jake exclaimed before almost slipping on a small sheet of ice. He let out a surprised yelp before Owen started talking.

"Really?" Owen asked sarcastically, tilting his head slightly. "I wouldn't think it would be... I mean, it's only-"

"Yeah yeah, enough." Jake huffed, his puff of breath floating upward and disappearing. "So, are we taking the truck?" He directed the conversation to Jack and Theo.

"We're just walking across the street to sleep for the night." Jack answered, his voice muffled because of the box covering his mouth.

"I'm guessing we're taking this to the sidewalk and coming back for the rest of the boxes?" Theo questioned, readjusting the boxes as he walked. Owen had to stop walking a couple times to keep the boxes from sliding down him and onto the ground.

"That's the plan." Jack nodded. "I was thinking of you all going back and leaving me with the boxes."

"I can stay with the boxes." Jake interjected. "In fact, I bet me and Owen could start taking them over."

"That would be dangerous." Jack started to state before Jake cut him off again.

"We'll be careful, I swear." He walked two steps to nudge Owen. "And I'd keep Owen safe no matter what."

"I don't need protecting." Owen mumbled.

"Just follow along." Jake muttered back, before keeping up with Jack's stride. "You guys will be back here in no time. See, we walked all the way down here in like what- a second?! C'mon, we can do it! Please?" He stared into Jack's eyes as he placed down the boxes on the sidewalk.

"Fine. I trust you boys." Jack gave in. "But if you two get hurt... just scream or something. I'll get down here as fast as I can."

"Got it. But we won't even need to do that because we'll be so careful." Jake insisted, which made Owen's stomach pause in its tracks. As he placed his boxes down beside Jake and Theo's, he thought about what Jake could possibly be thinking because he knew it couldn't be good.

"Ok..." Jack narrowed his lingering eyes at Jake before turning away and walking back up the parking lot.

"Be safe my boy." Theo hugged Owen before following Jack. Owen yawned, feeling his eyes droop as he leaned to pick up two boxes.

"Dude, you'll never guess what Jack said to me." Jake leaned over and also picked up two boxes. "We were walking down the hall, remember?"

"Yeah...?"

"And remember I said I'd go to the store with him?" Jake asked, not advancing to the sidewalk like Owen thought he would. He was a little louder now that they were out of hearing range.

"U-huh." Owen nodded, shifting his weight to his right foot while staring at him.

"He said that someone needs to stay with you at all times. To protect you from the monster or other weird things that might happen."

"What other things does he think will happen?" Owen asked, his heart jumping when a car raced by. He dropped a box and grabbed his shirt to try and stop his heart from hurting and thumping.

"How about you stay here and I run these across the street?" Jake asked. "Someone has to stay over here to watch for Jack and Theo. That, and the fact I'm faster." He added.

"You are not!" Owen retorted, kicking the box closer to the others and further from the road.

"Do you want me to stay over here then?" Jake questioned sarcastically.

"...no." Owen answered quietly, looking away from Jake and down at the boxes.

"Alright then... I'm right, you're wrong, and I'm running over." Jake didn't wait long enough for Owen to come up with a remark. Owen watched Jake run over with his two boxes, making his chest and throat shrink up. He quickly placed them down and started running back over. A car flickered into view and almost swerved into Jake. Owen let out the breath he was secretly holding, making his whole body shake. It didn't seem like Jake saw it, but he wasn't sure.

Jake paused to catch his breath. "Alright." Jake panted, placing his hands on his knees. He then reached down and picked up two more boxes. "Two boxes down. Some more to go." Jake proceeded to turn back to the road and do the same thing he did before, without almost being hit that time. Seeing Jake do it again and again and again made Owen feel a little more comfortable for his time to do it.

"Ok. Do you have these two if I take over this one?" Jake asked Owen.

"Yeah, I got it." Owen answered before turning away from the road to see if Jack and Theo were coming back. He saw them slowly making their way up, chatting and laughing the whole way. At least he hoped that's what they were doing. He could sometimes hear them and the closer they got, the easier it was to hear.

A loud horn blared behind him, shaking him to his very core. He whipped around to face what had caused it. Owen's body tensed and trembled seeing the sight that unfolded before him. Jake paused in his tracks and was slammed by the truck that flickered in and out of sight like something holographic. Jake's body fell over, as if knocked off balance instead of being hit straight on. Owen felt his legs run over to Jake and fall to his knees.

His hands reached down to touch Jake's limp body.

Owen shook Jake's body. "Jake, Jake get up please?" His quiet voice held a sense of urgency. After a few seconds of Jake not waking up, he tried to pick him up and drag him across the road. It felt and sounded like a few cars flew past them before his mind caught up to the horror that was about to happen. Owen looked up from Jake's pale face to see a silhouette of a car headed in their direction.

"NO!" Owen screamed, throwing his hands up in front of him. He closed his stinging eyes, waiting for the sudden pain to fill his body.

Chapter 6

Jake heard something close to him, though he couldn't really identify it. It sounded like he had his head underwater. He couldn't feel his body and he couldn't remember anything that happened after leaving the car dealership.

"Do you think... will affect his... body?" A very muffled and quiet voice asked from his left. He couldn't make out all the words, and some of them were a few guesses.

No response that he could hear.

"Do you... he'll... quickly?" The same voice asked, sounding more concerned than the first time.

Still no response.

Jake started to think something was seriously wrong with his hearing, but things slowly started to become clearer and tingling pain slowly started to seep in.

"Jack, seriously, this is going to keep us planted here for a few days at best." The voice, now recognizable as Theo's, stated. "We need to think about what his injuries are to prepare for the worst case scenarios. We can't wait any longer."

No noise came from Jack.

Jake tried his best not to move so he could continue to listen without being caught and so that the pain, that slowly took over his entire body, would stop. He wanted to figure out what happened to make him feel this way, and the more he listened, the better his chances were at learning it.

Theo sighed, then his voice shifted to Jake's right ear. "I understand this is what made you learn he existed, and..." Theo trailed off.

Jake's mind screamed, which didn't help his forming headache. He wanted to ask who they were talking about now, if it was him or someone else, but he wasn't ready to face the pain.

A deep sigh came from Jack. "That's not what I'm thinking about." He muttered, packing a slight emotional punch.

"...Then what?"

"I'm thinking about the worst case scenarios. One being he's in a coma, two being his entire body is paralyzed, and three being he's dead." Jack started to list, sounding more angry with each number listed.

"I'm positive he's not dead." Theo tried to insist, starting to sound concerned again.

"How do you know?" Jack blurted, though he kept his voice low. "This is all your fault that we're here."

"Now you know that's not true." Theo snapped, still sounding like he was trying to keep his emotions in check. "Maybe we should take a break from each other." Theo's voice got quieter. "And come back when we both calm down."

Jake heard Jack get up, stomping his foot down close to his body. "I'll go see how Owen is."

51

"And I'll stay here." Theo replied, his voice drifting away.

Jack stomped away and slammed a door while Theo's oddly quiet footsteps stopped close to his head.

Jake's attention slowly turned to the door, but quickly pivoted to the cold thing that just touched his head. His eyes did a weird twitch when it touched his eyebrows.

"Jack has to see that we have other things to worry about than what got us here." Theo muttered. "He has to learn that not everything goes in the direction you think it will." He stopped for a moment, the sound of shuffling was close to the top of Jake's head.

"I thought he learned that from his ex-wife." Theo sighed. "Dewling on that won't help us now. We need to figure out how we'll deal with my wife when we get out of here."

Jake heard the door handle twist and heard someone walk in. "Are you guys ok? It sounded like something fell in here." Owen asked, and Theo probably nodded.

Jake's eyes slid open, the dim light very unwelcoming to his eyes. He squeezed his eyes shut, only to make his head hurt more than it already did.

"Jake?" Theo questioned quietly, sounding very shocked. He cleared his throat. "I mean- Are you ok, son?" He asked as Owen walked over and sat down on the ground.

"Mmmh-." Jake groaned, his lips stuck together. After licking his very dry and cracked lips to try and bring life back into them, he mumbled. "Yeah."

Owen and Theo let out audible sighs of relief.

"Does anything hurt?" Theo asked, then Jake saw

something cover the light completely.

"Yeah." Jake mumbled.

"What is it?" Theo pressed, concerned.

"Everything." He whined, followed by a long sigh.

"That makes sense." Theo replied, not sounding as concerned as before. "But does anything hurt worse than everything else? And don't lie about it now."

"I don't know." Jake admitted. "My head? But it's starting to feel better now."

"Alright..." Theo's voice drifted off. Theo's silhouette uncovered the light. "Owen, can you go tell Jack that Jake's awake?"

Owen must have nodded, because Jake heard quieting footsteps then heard the door handle move and the door close.

"If you don't mind," Theo started, pausing a second. "I would like to check for any bruising anywhere."

"I don't care, check away." Jake shrugged. He felt Theo trying to take off his jacket and twisted a bit to help take it off. His arms throbbed lightly while doing it, but he let Theo place them on the ground beside him without complaining.

"Did that hurt at all?" Theo asked.

"It did, but it didn't hurt badly." Jake answered.

"Ok." Theo mumbled. "Is the ice helping?"

"Ice? Oh that's what the cold thing is." Jake realized. "Yeah, my head barely hurts at all anymore." He answered.

"Good, good." Theo said as he pulled Jake's sleeve up. Theo lifted Jake's arm, turning it around slowly before pulling the sleeve back down. Theo then slightly bended his elbow, taking Jake by surprise. "Does this hurt?" He quickly asked.

"No." Jake replied, shocked that he didn't feel any pain. He felt his arm bend, touch his shoulder, and slowly placed on the floor.

Theo did this with his other arm and his legs, getting the same response from Jake each time.

"Could you open your eyes for me, please?" Theo asked while taking off the shushy-ice off his head.

"Could you turn the lights off first?" Jake responded "I'm like, right under it." He explained.

"Of course, once Owen and Jack come back-" The door swung open and shut. "Good timing." Theo turned his head. "Could one of you please shut off the lights?"

Someone must have nodded because the light soon disappeared from his eyelids, allowing him to open up his eyes.

"Hey Owen, could you go out there and grab any pillows or blankets?" Theo asked.

Owen most likely nodded, opened the door and closed it behind him.

Jack sighed, looking at Jake as he laid there. Jake wanted to scream to Owen to hurry back. The tension was so thick he could practically see it lay on his chest to suffocate him.

"What you did back there was reckless." Jack finally said, his voice authoritative. He must have seen the mild confusion on his face because he added. "Owen told us what you were doing."

Jake felt as light as a feather when Jack said that. He didn't remember what he had done. But instead of asking, he just sighed. "I'm sorry."

"Apologies aren't going to make you any better." Jack looked toward Theo, then back to Jake. "I'm just glad you're ok." His voice mellowed out and he almost sounded relieved.

A less tension-filled silence followed. Jake wasn't sure what to say to that. He was relieved he was ok too. Jake just hoped Owen didn't take much longer with the blankets and pillows.

"So... earlier, before you woke up." Theo started. "Did you hear anything?" He asked.

Jake hesitated, wondering what he could mean by that. Jake did hear things, but they probably weren't something he should've heard.

Jake didn't have to think about it for too long, because the door swung open to reveal Owen. Or he hoped it was Owen underneath all of those Christmas themed blankets and pillows.

"Thank you Owen." Theo waved Owen over before helping Jack slowly help Jake sit up. Owen plopped the pillows and blankets on the ground behind Jake, then proceeded to make them taller. Jack and Theo slowly placed Jake's head down onto the tall fluffy mound.

"So, what are we doing now?" Jake asked when he settled himself in an unawkward position.

"What do you mean?" Theo returned a question.

"How are we going to fix all of this weird stuff going on? Or are we going to escape?" Jake asked. "I mean, if we are in this simulation thing."

"We're going to escape this simulation once you're up on your feet and feeling better." Theo answered, glancing at Jack before he continued. "The crazy weather has stopped and Jack's already brought over a truck big enough for all of us. We just have to work out the plan."

"The plan? What plan?" Jake asked, figuring out how much he missed after who knows how long.

"Our plan for us to escape." Theo started explaining.

"I already explained to Owen that we're looking for a tall silver building, like a skyscraper, only smaller." He shifted into a different sitting position. "At least, that's how it looked when we came here. We just have to hope nothing changes during that time."

"Changes?" Jake questioned. He had too many questions swarming his mind, but that was the first one that escaped his mouth.

"Yes... well... we've noticed that- um-." Theo stopped for a second, staring off to the distance like the words were plastered somewhere on the walls. "This world is gradually shifting... maybe even moving around. We're not sure." "Jack brought it to our attention when he almost lost the pharmacy. I'm afraid if we don't act soon, Jack and I won't be able to find our way back."

"It's not far from here." Jack informed Jake, who was looking through his internal map of the places he'd been. Jake must not have gone close to the building because it wasn't showing up on his map. "We just have to be careful." Jack stressed.

"The word of the week." Jake mumbled and everyone nodded their agreement.

"So." Theo broke the silence. "I guess you must be hungry. Would you like us to get you something to eat?" Jack and Theo stood up before Jake could answer. "We'll let you and Owen talk. I know you're probably dying to talk to him." Theo walked to the door and Jack slowly followed behind. "See you in a minute." Jack shut the door behind them.

Jake gave the adults time to walk off before turning to Owen. "Owen. You'll never guess what I overheard."

Owen scooted closer, keeping his voice low. "What?"

"Jack and Theo were fighting before Jack talked to you." Jake paused for a second to remember what he heard. "They brought up something about this accident, that's how Jack knew someone existed."

"Really?" Owen pulled one of his hands off the floor and changed his position.

"Yeah." Jake said with surprise in his tone. "Then Jack tried to blame the fact we're here is because of Theo. And then they decided it was best for them to take a break from each other. That's when Jack went to talk to you."

Owen's wide eyes were glued on Jake, so he decided to continue.

"But when he left, Theo started talking about how Jack can't worry about what got them here. And something about Jack having an ex-wife."

"Jack didn't talk to me. I went to see what happened in here." Owen explained.

"Jack slammed the door." Jake answered, feeling himself slowly slide down the pillows and blankets propped against the wall. "He sounded very upset. But enough about that, what did you hear?"

"What do you mean?" Owen raised an eyebrow.

"While I was out. What happened?" Jake reworded.

"Nothing really." Owen shrugged. "You were only out for two days-."

"Two days!" Jake blurted. "What happened that caused me to be out for two days?!"

"You know." Owen scrunched his eyebrows together. Jake stared at him blankly. "You got hit by a car?" He questioned sarcastically.

Jake nodded, pushing himself upright. "That's right." He breathed.

Owen shook his head. "How could you possibly

forget that?"

"Enough about that." Jake waved his hand at Owen. "Tell me what happened. I want to know if I can link the things I heard to the things you heard."

"Ok… all I heard was them talking about the plan yesterday." Owen recalled. "Jack was out getting the truck. I was here with Theo, trying to get more supplies. Oh, we found bags."

"Cool." Jake nodded.

"That's basically it." Owen continued. "No fighting, no more weird weather, and no monster."

"Well that's always-."

Jack and Theo burst into the room out of breath. Both of them were carrying at least seven backpacks, one on their backs, one on their chest, and the rest hung from their arms. Jake felt his heart jump as Jack walked over and glared down at him.

"Jake, can you stand?" Jack asked, his voice harsh.

"Yeah, I can try." Jake slowly got to his shaky feet as he listened to Owen and Theo.

"What's going on?" Owen mumbled.

"The monster's coming." Theo explained. "We saw it near the dealership."

"The dealerships back?" Owen asked.

"No time to explain everything now, we have to go before it gets here." Theo handed Owen five bags from his arms, then gestured for Jack and Owen to go first.

Jake walked over to Theo, his body feeling weak from not using it.

"The car's up at the front." Theo explained while they walked out and down the hallway. "You get in front of me and I'll help you from behind."

"Ok." Jake walked out of the small, employees-only, hall and through the dark and quiet pharmacy. The only light came from the small windows near the ceiling and the sliding doors. Jake didn't walk slow, but he wasn't sprinting either. He thought about how he'd be the reason they'd be caught by the monster.

They got to the sliding doors and saw the truck up on the concrete, doors open and ready for them to climb in. The doors slid open and Theo helped Jake climb into the truck before getting in himself. Owen reached over Jake and shut the door just as Jack slammed on the gas and shot out from the brick overhang and back onto the black asphalt.

"Did you see the monster?" Theo struggled to buckle his seatbelt.

"No." Jack answered. "I figure heading to the building will-."

Owen turned around in his seat to look behind them. "It's at the pharmacy!" Owen shouted.

Theo and Jake turned to look at the monster. As soon as Jake locked eyes with it, the pharmacy, and the monster vanished, leaving behind a straight piece of road unconnected with the piece they were on.

Chapter 7

Owen practically gasped when the pharmacy disappeared, Jack on the other hand just kept gunning it. He sped on without giving what just happened a second thought. Owen knew that was for the best, they couldn't doddle anymore. They need this possible advantage.

"Jack, slow down." Theo insisted.

"Who knows where that thing ended up. It could be in front of us for all we know." Jack pointed out. "And if we keep moving, there's a less chance of us getting teleported or whatnot."

"You have good points." Theo reluctantly sighed. He pulled the bags off of his arms and placed them in the back with Owen and Jake, along with the others. Owen's feet were buried in the backpacks, glueing them to the ground.

"What will we do once we get to the building?" Jake asked, pulling his seatbelt over him. "Actually, what does this building even do?" Jake cut Theo off before he even opened his mouth.

Jack was the first to respond. "The building is what will get us out of this simulation and into the real world. It's where we appeared when we entered this whole place." He explained. "This building won't be the problem, the real one will be the real problem." He added quietly.

"Yes. There are people in the real world guarding the whole building." Theo joined in.

"Why?" Jake asked. Owen just stayed silent and listened.

"Because..." Theo quickly paused. "It's a very highly populated place filled with rich and famous people, along with expensive equipment. There's never been a single break-in, and we'd like to keep it that way."

Jake thought for a moment. "We?" He questioned.

Theo let out a deep sigh, but before he could speak, Jack responded.

"We had to work there and get close to the boss in order to get into the room." Jack answered. The more answers Owen listened to, the more questions he got. This whole thing was confusing. Why did they have to get close with the boss if they were in the simulation? It feels like they already knew the boss. But did the boss put them in, or was it someone else? Owen paused for a moment when he watched Jake open his mouth again.

"Did you help put us in here?"

Jake's question silenced everyone. The only sound was the car zooming down the road. No one spoke for what felt like ages. Owen didn't even think that far. The more time he spent with them, the more he felt like he knew them, but now he felt like he was in a car with strangers. The silence stretched on and on, and Owen looked out the window. He didn't want to wrap his mind around the worst possible answer his mind always thought of first. He watched the sun reach the peak in the sky before someone spoke again.

"We can't lie." Theo finally told Jack, very quietly. Jack huffed, but didn't verbally protest. Theo didn't look back at them when he answered with a painstakingly quiet. "Yes."

Owen felt like his body tumbled out of the car and hit a tree. He couldn't believe it. He stared blankly out the window, unblinking. They were saving them but they also put them in this mess? What sick people would put kids in a weird contraption, then suddenly change their mind? His mouth hung open, his mind spinning and swirling before catching onto Jake's question.

"Why...?" Jake was uncharacteristically quiet. For a while, Owen thought Jack and Theo didn't hear the question. Theo didn't look back at them, Jack didn't even glance into the rear-view mirror. Both of them were silent and unmoving.

The long, dead quiet was broken by small sobs from Theo. "You have to believe us boys, this wasn't our fault." He pleaded, but didn't look back at them. "We didn't choose to do this."

"Sure you didn't." Jake muttered, folded his arms, and glared at the bag-filled floor.

Theo turned back and stared at them through tears, trying to explain. "I swear on my life it didn't even cross our minds to do this." He insisted.

"Then who's mind did it cross?" Jake asked harshly.

"It was his psycho wife's idea." Jack spat. "She even did it without telling us she was doing it." He continued. "She came up with this idea of a show and movie-making software thing, then decided how nice it would be to have her son as the main character."

"Me?" Owen mumbled, pointing at himself with a shaky hand. His words barely made it out of his mouth.

Theo nodded. "I told her... I wanted no part of it." He wiped his eyes with his hands. "I just wanted... to raise my son... and- and give him a loving family." He mumbled between gasps and quiet sobs. Owen's heart hurt and his eyes glossed over with tears as he listened.

"Your mother's sick in the head." Jack objected. "She's manipulative and cruel. The reason she had to come up with that whole project was because no one wanted to work with someone as psycho as her." Owen was more shocked and upset than anything. He wiped his eyes and nose with his sleeve. Jake reached over and placed a hand on Owen's shoulder.

Jake waited a moment before asking. "So... we're being recorded right now?" He wasn't crying, but he was visibly upset for Owen.

Theo took a second to try and compose himself. "More than likely." He took a shaky breath, his tears stopped for now but his eyes were still glossy. He moved to sit normally in his seat. "Knowing her, she's loving this." He added quietly.

Owen watched Jack as he took a few sharp turns on the winding road they were on. He finally slowed down, not to a normal speed, but enough that Owen felt left shaky and on edge. His hands still shook, his eyes occasionally had tears fall, and his breathing wasn't fully normal, but it was close enough. Owen didn't fully realize that he wasn't listening until he caught Jake ask another question.

"Then why am I in here?" Jake asked, shifting in his seat semi-uncomfortably. "And what about the monster, and these weird glitches? Is this world unstable or something?" Jake paused but quickly added. "But answer the first question first."

Both Theo and Jack seemed hesitant to answer, more than they usually were. Theo looked over at Jack, who gripped the wheel with white knuckles. Jack didn't look over at Theo, but grumbled something under his breath. Theo shook his head and sighed.

Owen and Jake turned to look at each other, sharing the same confused and worried glance.

"Jake... the reason you're here." Theo started, staring at the far off trees passed the yellow-green grass. "Is because..." Theo looked at the radio. Owen looked at the garbled shapes that were supposed to be numbers. "It's because..." Theo shook his head.

"Jake, you're dead." Jack bluntly forced it from his mouth. "Some stupid drunk driver hit you and your mother." He didn't look back as his words shot out of his mouth and his hands gripped the wheel. "She died, and you were going to be pronounced braindead." As Jack kept explaining, the car sped up faster and faster until everything that shot by was indistinguishable. "But Theo's *stupid* and *crazy* wife figured out we could preserve you in code!" Jack was nearly shouting by now. "I didn't say no. In fact, *I* just learned you *existed*!" He spat through gritted teeth. He sucked air through his teeth and calmed down slightly, releasing the gas some.

"Your body's still out there on life support." Theo explained quietly and calmly. "But your consciousness is in here."

Owen looked over at Jake, who looked visibly shaken to his core. His mouth hung open and his expression was blank as he sat there. For a good while, Jake just sat there. Owen placed a hand on his shoulder, offering the same quiet support Jake gave him a few minutes back. Jake's eyes started welling with tears but he just blinked them away. Jake started to nod slowly. "Ok." He mumbled, letting out a shaky breath. "And… the other questions?" Jake asked slowly and quietly, way out of character for him.

"Don't worry, once we get to the building and get ourselves back into the real world, you'll get back in your body." Theo explained softly. "Sense you're on life support, your body is alive."

Jake dramatically sighed and still looked scared. "Well that's good, at least I'm not entirely dead." He melodramatically joked, his eyes wide with shock. Owen slowly pulled his arm back after Jake's outburst.

Jake gave himself a second to breathe. "What if something goes wrong, or what if it-." Jake sighed, for real this time, and calmed himself down. "What about the other questions?" He quietly asked.

- -_-_-_-_-_-

Owen listened to Jack and Theo reluctantly answer Jake's questions. Supposedly Owen was supposed to have powers and the monster should've been confined to a cave. Apparently, sense the code corrupted or something, it managed to escape? He wasn't exactly sure about that. It was also supposed to be a dragon cat thing, a large, orange, tiger cat thing with back scales and stripes. The code corruption is slow, but they also expect his mom to be causing a few things. So one of the two is why weird things keep happening, like the teleporting buildings and the weird ghost people. Owen could not wrap his head around him having another mother or father. Theo could say it all he wants, he'll always see Mary and Eric as his mom and dad, no matter how much Owen has to go through.

As he took in all the information, he looked out of the window. As they drove he watched the hills change to meadows then change to trees that moved further from the road to reveal houses the longer they drove. First it was a few speckled houses here and there, some swallowed by trees, others in small communities similar to theirs. Then stores, gas stations, schools, and larger buildings started to appear, until that was all there was. Large buildings seemingly ate the plants and replaced them with sidewalks, gated communities, and apartment buildings.

"We're close boys." Jack announced. His once quick paced driving was now slow and more precise. "Be on the lookout for anything."

"Can one of you hand me a bottle of water from a bag?" Theo asked, reaching his hand out behind him.

"Yeah." Owen mumbled and reached down to zip open a bag. He pulled out a water bottle that sat on the top of everything else and handed it to Theo.

"Thank you." Theo thanked Owen and pulled his arm back up.

"Is the building going to look like all of these?" Jake asked while taking a small bag of cheez-its from Owen's bag. "It'll be like finding a haystack in a needle."

Everyone, even Jack, turned to stare at him with confusion.

"What?" Owen asked sarcastically. Jack turned back at the road and shook his head with a sigh.

"You know, finding a haystack in a needle?" Jake restated. "Don't tell me you haven't heard it before?"

"Finding a *haystack* in a *needle*?" Owen emphasized, furrowing his eyebrows in mild confusion.

"Yeah." Jake nodded. "It means you're trying to find something hard, right?"

"The saying is finding a *needle* in a *haystack*." Jack said in monotone.

Jake looked over at Owen with a raised eyebrow and a questioning expression.

"Yeah dude, it's true." Owen answered.

Jake kept staring at Owen. "Why would someone try to find a needle in a haystack?"

"How could someone even try finding a haystack in a needle, that's impossible?!" Owen retorted.

"It's a metaphor, Jake." Theo answered, turning to look at him. "It goes, needle in a haystack. And no one's actually going to look for a needle in a haystack."

"Oh…" Jake mumbled, looking down at his bag of cheez-its.

"Ok, are you three looking for the building? Or is it just me?" Jack asked, forcefully pulling themself off the subject.

"We're looking." Theo sighed, turning his head to look out his window.

"While we're looking." Jake started. "What's the plan for when we get out of this simulation? Are we going to set it on fire? We should set it on fire."

"No one's setting anything on fire." Theo cut Jake off.

"Dang it." Jake folded his arms and looked out his window.

"We're just simply going to run." Theo answered.

"I thought we were going to get the police involved?" Jack inquired quietly.

"Yes, but think about her position." Theo started. "More than likely, she's already pinned us to a fault. Also, look at the people who work for her. Would they take our word over theirs?" Jack shook his head. "But more importantly-." He got too quiet for Owen to hear what they were talking about. Owen proceeded to staring out his window and letting their conversation go in one ear and out the other.

"Then where do we run to?" Jack asked. "It's not like we have a secret place to hide out until we get some kind of evidence."

"Guys! Is that it?" Jake cut them off while pointing out the window to a grey building. It almost had no windows, only at the bottom, and even then they looked tinted. It wasn't huge, but it was close to the size of the dealership, but rectangle-shaped and boring.

"That's it." Theo answered. Jack turned the wheel down the road leading to the opening of the building. "Now, let's get out of here."

Chapter 8

Jake leapt out of his seat when they parked near the doors. There were no cars in the parking lot from what he could tell, but he wasn't focused on that at all. Jake was still stunned at the fact that they were talking about him. He listened to them talk while they thought he was still passed out. That whole, "this is how you met him" thing, it was about him. Jack didn't even know him... well, they were split up. Did they split up before he was even born? How old was he in the accident?

They all walked through the doors and into the building. Everyone was radiating nervousness and excitement, including him. He was never going to admit it, but he was scared something was going to happen. Jake didn't think they were going to make it this far without another incident.

"Alright, is anyone tired? The sun's going down." Theo peered out the window while Jack looked around the small lobby-looking area. So far, this reminded Jake of a pediatrician's office. It had the same weird glass windows and the same area for seating.

"A little." Owen admitted quietly. He was closer to Jake than he normally was.

"I am too." Jake hung an arm around Owen. "Are we going to sleep in here?"

"I'm thinking so." Jack walked around the dark, dull, and gray room. "The sky looks like it's getting cloudy again. And if this building were to teleport, saying it could teleport with people inside, then we don't have to worry about chasing it down."

"We should go and grab the bags then." Theo added. "We haven't needed them badly so far, but I don't want to be left defenseless if we do need them."

"That's what I was thinking." Jack nodded, walking to the door to stand beside Theo.

"You both find a place to sleep for the night." Jack opened the door, letting Theo out before adding. "I'd suggest somewhere close to the middle of the building, just in case." Then he walked out with Theo.

Jake turned to Owen. "Alright dude, let's find a place for us to sleep." He walked past the door before realizing that Owen was slowly dragging his feet. He looked shaky and disoriented.

"Bro, are you ok?" Jake asked, taking a step toward him. He knew he wasn't ok, even before Owen nodded his head.

"Yeah." Owen mumbled, picking up his pace but he was still sluggish compared to Jake.

Jake hesitated for a moment before walking again. He wasn't going to bring it up. If something was wrong, he was sure Owen would tell him. Still, he glanced back at Owen every time they'd pass a door. Jake felt like he was in a fever dream, it didn't feel real at all to him. He's dead? He looked back at Owen. How could he not remember dying, or anything from the real world? He looked back at Owen before turning a corner. He hated the idea he was

70

being watched. Even now, as they tried to escape their digital prison. He looked back at Owen, who just turned the corner. He tried his best not to think about it and instead looked at the rooms for a possible place to rest for the night. He looked back at Owen, only to realize he was frozen in place. Owen's hands were gripping his shirt and his whole body practically trembled. His breathing was quick and shallow. Jake froze, unsure what to do, but quickly shoved back his fear and walked over to Owen.

Jake gripped Owen's shoulders. "Dude, it's ok." Was the first thing he could come up with. Why was Owen freaking out? "We're safe." Was he scared about what will happen tomorrow? "Just breathe, alright?" He was trying to think. Both of them never had a panic attack before, and he wasn't the best at confort. "Uh- count to three when you breathe in and six when you breathe out?" He used that to sleep sometimes, when he was kept awake by his thoughts. Jake saw some improvement and felt Owen pull his arms around him. Jake did the same, feeling way out of his element. "See dude, you're good." He kept trying to figure out what he could do. He kept coming up with jokes but this wasn't the time for that.

"Everything keeps falling apart." Owen mumbled, snuffling. Jake could feel tears fall through his jacket and onto his shirt. "It just keeps coming... and coming..." Jake thought he was calming down for a moment but he just became more verbal? He continued to try and help. He nodded and continued to listen when Owen talked in between sobs. "I don't... know... what to do..." He said in between gasps. Jake was thinking the same thing, for all the situations. He was both confused and worried about Owen, but he wasn't sure what he could do.

"You'll feel better when we rest." Jake reluctantly

said, trying his best not to sound like he was reluctantly saying it. "You're just pumped up on adrenaline. C'mon." He shuffled Owen into the next room he found, which was actually perfect. It looked like a small lounge, with two long couches placed in the center of the room around a table. Jake helped Owen sit beside him, not letting him go. Owen placed his forehead on his shoulder and Jake just sat there. He was still confused, but he figured if he got Owen to sleep he'd feel better.

After what felt like ages, Jake heard soft snoring and Owen's grip softened. He slowly and carefully leaned Owen back onto the round armrest of the couch. He placed his head onto it before anxiously attempting to pull his legs up onto the rest of the couch. After the successful attempt, Jake plopped himself onto the other couch. He pulled his feet up, not taking his shoes off, and closed his eyes. He felt the tug of sleep pulling at his body when he got comfortable. His mind didn't wander far before the pull tugged him into sleep.

-_-_-_-_-_-

Jake felt something shaking his shoulder. Then he felt something pull his leg until he fell head-first onto the carpeted, yet hard, floor.

"Ow!" Jake exclaimed, pushing himself upright as the thing let go of his leg. He glared at the person who dragged him out of bed or off of couch.

"C'mon dude." Owen stood upright.

"...what?" Jake yawned, placing his head on the ground.

"Get up." Owen kicked Jake on the leg. Jake just rolled over and faced the couch, his face pressed against it.

"No." Jake muffled, placing a hand under his head and preparing to sleep again. He wasn't even tired, he just didn't want to get up yet.

"Fine." Owen gave up and it sounded like he walked away. "I guess I'll just eat these Funyuns all by myself."

Jake shoved himself off the floor. "Ok maybe I'm not tired." He quickly decided, holding his arms straight out and signaled with his hands for Owen to give him some.

"No no, you're tired, I get it." Owen shrugged, earning a scowl from Jake. His hands dropped to his side.

"Dude, give me the Funyuns." Jake told him as Owen walked over to the bags. Jack and Theo must have dropped them off while they were asleep.

Owen picked one up and grabbed a bag of Funyuns out of it. "Fine, here." He threw it over to Jake, who gratefully caught it and dug in. Owen walked over to him and sat on the couch beside Jake.

"So what's the plan?" Jake asked, pushing himself up onto the couch with the bag by his teeth.

"They'll probably get us sooner than later. I haven't seen them since last night." Owen explained, leaning back. "I just have this feeling dude."

"Not a feeling." Jake sarcastically joked while shoving a Funyon in his mouth. Owen gave him an annoyed glance and Jake held up his hands. "Ok, continue." He ate another Funyun.

"I can't even understand it." Owen admitted.

"Dude, I don't even feel like this is real." Jake started explaining. "This whole thing doesn't feel real to me. You know that weird dream thing you can do? It's something like liquid dreaming."

"Lucid?" Owen guessed.

"Lucid dreaming! That's it." Jake nodded, pointing a Funyun at Owen before eating it. "It just feels like a sick and messed up lucid dream."

"Like, we know our friends and families are gone. It just seems too bizarre to even think-."

"Exactly!" Jake agreed. "You'd think we'd at least remember something about our life before being put in here."

"What if we were too young to remember?" Owen breathed.

Both of them paused for a moment and let it stir and simmer.

"Nope, too deep and serious." Jake broke the silence. "That's not us dude."

Jake and Owen laughed for a while before sighing and leaning against the back of the couch again.

"Ok, the monster." Jake shot up. "You have powers?"

"What do those two sentences have in common?" Owen asked.

"I don't know, Theo used them together." Jake shrugged.

"I don't think I'm flying around and shooting lasers out of my eyes." Owen

"I wish Theo could tell us when danger is near again." Owen mumbled.

"First, where did that come from? Second, what do you mean?" Jake asked before eating another Funyun.

"The same place you got the monster and superpowers." Owen retorted. "Anyway, Theo was the voice I was hearing." He recalled. "I asked him while we were at the pharmacy."

"Huh." Jake ate another Funyun. "Who knew." He mumbled. Honestly, he forgot all about the fact Owen went crazy and started hearing voices.

"Speaking of Theo. He's my dad?"

"You *just* got that?" Jake questioned sarcastically. "After the whole car dealership thing?"

"Not like that." Owen rolled his eyes. "Like, believing it wise."

"Ohhh, ok. Yeah, I don't get it." Jake admitted. "Like, Mary and Eric were your parents. But then again, Jack's my dad."

"Honestly, I'm surprised he didn't say that specifically at the dealership." Owen added. "Theo said he was mine, but all he said was you were related to him."

"Maybe back then it felt too complicated to say it?" Jake guessed. "Maybe Jack didn't believe it himself?"

"Maybe." Owen mumbled. "It must be great for you to have a sort of father figure now, saying..."

"Eric and Theo feel more like dad's to me than Jack. Jack kind of feels like a steel block than a person." Jake shrugged. "But hey, he's better than my parents. At least he's actually here and he seems to care." Jake's smile faded slightly but popped back. "Do we want to see what Jack and Theo are doing?" He asked, standing up.

"Sure." Owen shrugged and hopped off the couch. They both walked through the door and down the hall to the front.

"Do you know where they are?" Jake and Owen stopped walking for a second, both still eating their Funyuns.

"No. I figured we'd walk to the front and see if they're there." Owen explained.

"Ok, that makes sense." Jake agreed and they

both started walking again. They saw the light shooting through the window. But the way it was tucked behind the buildings didn't make it possible for the sun to come through the windows. Jake shrugged it off, until they walked to the front and looked through the tinted doors and windows.

"Dude?" Owen whispered, looking over at Jake with wide eyes. "Why are we in a grassy field?"

Both of them were silent for a while. Owen was slightly sitting on the windowsill with his back leaning up against it. Jake was pacing.

"Oh my gosh! It poofed!" Jake turned toward Owen, his heart beating quicker.

"Poofed? You mean teleported?" Owen reworded.

"Yeah, yeah whatever." Jake waved Owen away and shifted his weight to his left leg. "Just like the pharmacy did, and the car dealership." He folded his arms.

"So we're in the middle of nowhere!" Owen exclaimed, jumping off the windowsill. "What do we do!"

"I don't know! We can't leave without them, we don't know how!" Jake quickly added. "We can't leave this place, because then it might poof away without us!"

"So we just sit here and hope and pray the monster doesn't come and eat us? Better yet, we hope we don't teleport to an ocean or something?!" Owen seemed to feed off Jake's rising anxiety. He needed to calm them down, for both of their sakes. Someone needed to keep their head.

"How about this." Jake started, walking down the hallway again with Owen close behind. He walked into the room they were in and started picking up backpacks. "We take these and get up high somewhere to just wait out and hide. That way the monster has a long way to get to us, and we're out of other harm's way too."

Owen nodded. "Sounds good." He agreed, also starting to pick up backpacks. At the end, Jake had four backpacks and Owen had two.

They walked back to the front and looked around for a possible stairway.

"This says exit, maybe the stairway's there too?" Owen pointed out. It led back down the hallway, but kept going straight until the very end.

"Ok. I'll lead the way." Jake walked forward and they both started their trek down the hallway. It was the only light in the entire building, despite there being large and long lights down the hallways. They got to the end and it turned right. "This way." He mumbled and continued walking until they were met with a metal door.

"Stairs!" They both exclaimed. Jake opened the door and let Owen inside first.

"It's so cold in here." Owen stated.

"Well, it is all concrete." Jake explained. "That, and it's close to outside." He gestured to a glass door with his foot, leading toward a thick line of trees.

"Whatever man, let's keep going." Owen sighed and started up the stairs. Everything echoed in the stairwell, from their loud footsteps to their breathing. Jake's body started to hurt once they got to the first platform. His leg muscles felt like they were being pulled tighter the longer they kept going up. His heart pointed in his head, making it hurt. Jake felt dizzy but still pulled himself up the stairs by clinging onto the railing. He looked up the winding staircase.

"Are we there yet?" Jake called up to Owen, who was already two flights of stairs ahead.

"Yeah, I think so." Owen replied. "Why, you getting

tired?" He sarcastically asked, looking down at him.

Jake leaned against the railing. "Nah dude, I'm fine. Let's keep going." Jake started walking up the stairs. Owen hesitated before going back to walking.

Chapter 9

Owen climbed up the stairs, his legs starting to feel exhausted after the sixth staircase. He was starting to think this staircase went on forever until he got to the eighth one.

"There are no more stairs, just a door." Owen informed Jake, who was now three staircases away. Owen leaned over the railing to look down at Jake to see what he was saying.

"Ok." Jake replied in a very whispered tone, almost as if he was trying to catch his breath. "Do you want to go ahead and look around up there?" He stopped walking and leaned on the railing that was on the platform.

"I'll just wait for you." Owen answered. First, he didn't want to let Jake be alone because he knew if he did, he'd faint from the panic. He didn't feel all shaky and scared now, but he didn't want the chance for it to happen. Second, he wanted to stay in case Jake finally admitted he needed help.

"Alright." Jake pushed himself off the railing and started to drag himself up the stairs.

"Are you sure you're ok?" Owen asked as he watched Jake struggle up the fifth staircase. His legs were shaking when he took one off the stair and onto the other.

"Yeah, I'm good. I'm just still tired, that's all." Jake lied. Owen rolled his eyes and sighed.

"Sure looks like you're good, dude." Owen shot back. "Seriously man. If you're tired, take a break."

"I'm almost there." Jake insisted. "I'll take a break once we find a room."

Owen looked up at the wall, his head drooped with his arms holding him up on the railing. It was only a day ago when Jake woke up from that weird coma thing. Even though he wasn't hurting then, or he didn't tell them he was, it was obvious that he was hurting now. He was overexerting himself. Owen reluctantly shrugged it off, twisting to lean his back on the railing, his legs folded over each other. Owen knew Jake would do the same thing.

Owen waited for a good five minutes before Jake finally reached the top of the stairs. When he got up there, he loudly sighed, the noise echoing off the walls. He leaned against the wall and looked over at Owen.

"What are we waiting for? Let's get going." Jake slowly jumped off the wall and opened the door beside him. Owen sighed, stood upright, and walked through the door.

This hallway actually had windows, unlike the ones downstairs. It made the dark gray everything look more bright. Owen wondered if the whole building looked the same in the real world, monochrome, bland, void of life.

"How about down here?" Owen suggested the first hallway they came across to Jake, who was closer to the wall than he normally was.

"Whatever works, as long as we're closer to the

middle." Jake replied. They both slowly walked down the hallway. Out of the corner of Owen's eye, he saw Jake stumble slightly. Jake quickly regained his balance and continued walking. Owen felt his throat try to close and his palms started to sweat. They had to find a room before Jake made himself collapse. Owen found a door and barged in. It swung open without any noise and led them to a weird meeting room. The room had large, black rolly chairs on every side of a long rectangle table close to the size of the room. It looked like there was a projector hanging from the ceiling, and there were no windows or lights on, as usual.

Owen walked around the room and sat in one of the chairs. They were surprisingly plush and comfortable despite their disproportionate size. Jake walked in behind him and sat in the nearest chair. He sunk into the chair and let out a sigh of relief.

"Dude! These chairs are awesome." Jake's toes were the only thing touching the ground. Owen was shocked because Jake was taller than him, only by a few inches that didn't really count, but still. Owen pushed himself into the chair completely, his back feeling the back of the seat.

"They really are." Owen sounded a little surprised. He watched Jake squirm around until his legs dangled off one arm rest and his back was up against another.

- - - - - - - - - -

Owen and Jake sat there in silence for a while. Jake even managed to fall asleep in the chair. Owen sat there half asleep with his legs propped up on the table. Even though he had a good amount of sleep last night, he couldn't help his eyelids slowly starting to slide down his eyes. His breathing slowed down and he felt relaxed. Owen's eyelids now covered his eyes completely. He felt himself fall asleep and he thought nothing would ever be able to get him out of that chair.

Owen heard a door slam and was unable to tell if it was now open or closed. Owen shot up, falling out of the chair and onto the floor, his legs caught on the table. The loud noises woke Jake as Owen fumbled to get himself to his feet.

"What's going on?" Jake asked, still groggy from sleeping.

"A door slammed." Owen answered quickly.

Jake thought for a moment before getting off the chair. "Under the table." He motioned before grabbing his chair and pulling it close to the table. Owen did the same, crouching under the table while pulling his chair as far as it could. They slowly crawled to the end of the table and curled into themselves, trying to get smaller.

"Jake, Owen!" It sounded like Jack, but Jake and Owen didn't move. "Boys! Are you up here?!" He sounded different... panicked? Maybe. Owen wasn't too sure. He didn't want to come out and have it somehow be the monster mimicking his voice.

Jack's footsteps walked to their room, his blue jeans and work boots the only things they could see. "Answer me!" His legs walked into the room and he started pulling chairs out. "Don't be dead." He muttered under his breath.

Both boys untangled themselves from their ball forms and crawled out from under the table. After that whole incident, Owen felt a little tired, but it was nothing he couldn't get over.

82

Jack looked relieved, the first emotion he showed other than anger or annoyance. He quickly helped them up to their feet. He hugged them both, burying their heads into his body. "When you hear someone calling your name that you know, you answer." He told them, but his tone wasn't upset.

"Ok." Owen heard Jake's muffled answer.

Jack sighed and let them go. "I'm just glad you two are ok." He mumbled quickly before turning around, folding his arms, and clearing his throat. "You both had Theo worried sick." He didn't look at them, but Owen knew Jack really cared too.

"Where is he?" Jake asked.

"Downstairs." Jack replied before walking to the door. "In case the monster showed up." He added as everyone walked down the hall and to the stairway.

"Not the stairs again!" Jake jokingly whined. Owen wasn't sure if he was truly joking or trying to joke because he really didn't want to walk the stairs again.

"You two don't have to walk all of them again, the system thing is on the third floor." Jack explained. Owen glanced at the plaque next to the door before walking down the stairs. Garbled garbage was what it read, perfect. The white supposed words and the black plaque looked like a marble slab.

Jack must have seen it too, because he added. "It's just underneath us."

"Alright." Jake shrugged, moving more smoothly and quickly down the stairs than before. That made Owen feel a little better.

Owen walked down the stairs behind them. They're finally getting out. All their problems were going to be solved. No more monster, no more teleporting, no more ghost cars or people. Everything is so close to being normal again. They just have to get out, arrest his mother or something, and then everything's normal. They made it to the platform, just about to open the door.

Everyone jumped when they heard the door slam open and echo. "Jack!" A scream came from downstairs. "Jack! You found them, yes?!" It was Theo, he sounded frantic. It sounded like he started running up the stairs.

"Yes, Theo! What is it?" Jack responded.

"The monster's close! I'm not sure if it spotted me, but it'll find its way here!" Theo explained, his running echoed off the walls along with everything else.

"Ok." Jack answered as he turned to look at them. "You two first." He opened the door for them, gesturing quickly to go inside. Jake and Owen ran in but quickly paused. They didn't know where to go. Owen's heartbeat quickened, he felt it in his chest as his legs tried to hold his entire shaking body. Jake was standing in front of him slightly, watching the door.

Theo ran through and nearly tackled Owen. His arms wrapped around him and Theo almost picked him off the ground. "I'm so glad you two are ok!" His tears fell onto Owen's clothing. Theo removed one arm and wrapped it around Jake.

Jack's footsteps came up behind them. "I don't want to break this up, but let's get going." Jack walked past them and walked down the halls.

Theo let them go and wiped his tears. "C'mon, boys." He walked off and Jake and Owen quickly followed behind.

"So how will this work?" Jake asked, catching up with Theo. "Are we going to get poked with needles or something?"

"We'll sit in chairs." Theo started. Owen listened to them talk and watched his feet carry him to the room. "There are wires that attach to our temples." He tapped where they were on his head, but didn't look back at them. "Then, we'll close our eyes and we'll be in the space between the real word and the simulation."

"That's confusing." Jake bluntly stated.

Owen's body was jittery with anxiety and his mind started to shut down.

"Are we just sleeping? Will we be able to open our eyes and be back here? Will we see each other there?" Jake blurted out questions. Owen felt that now wasn't the time at all, and didn't dare say anything. Jack sped off, leaving them with just Theo, who seemed to know the way by heart.

"I don't know." Theo admitted. "We just came and went, we didn't dottle or dilly dally."

"What is that going to look like?" Jake asked.

"Dark." Theo answered. "I don't remember a lot about it."

"Do we appear in there for a second then show up in the real world? How does it work?"

"We'll walk until we see a white door that glows." Theo tried to explain while keeping his pace. "What I think it is, is we're in a limbo where the simulation and the real world meet up for people to cross over. We walk through the glowing fixture and end up in our real bodies."

"Ok." Jake gave in. Owen watched Jake slow down slightly, keeping Owen's pace. They kept following Theo, Jake's steady pace starting to falter. They turned a corner and saw Jack stand in front of large doors that reminded Owen of gym doors. Jack pulled one of them open for them.

"Get in." Jack continuously waved his arm to the room and they all quickly filled in. "Choose a chair to sit in." Jack told them, walking over to the several computer monitors up against a wall. Owen let Jake sit in the first one, then sat beside him in the next one. Owen's mind couldn't process anything, he could barely feel the chair he sat in. He focused hard on listening to them talk.

Theo walked behind the chairs and handed Jake a blue and red wire with white tape stuff on the ends. "The red one goes on your right temple and the blue one goes on your left." He explained while handing Owen his. He then walked over and sat in the chair beside Owen. As Owen got his, he watched Jake make L's with his hand, then switched which wire was in which hand. Owen's shaky hands fumbled with the wires, almost dropping them and sticking them wrong.

Jack did something with the computers before walking over to Jake. He knelt down beside him and whispered in his ear Owen couldn't hear. He then watched Jack stand up and he thought he saw Jack start to tear up. He watched Jack forcefully blink before he spoke.

"Ok. Everyone ready?" Jack asked.

Everyone nodded.

"Good." Jack walked over to his chair and put the tape on the sides of his head.

Jake turned to look at Owen. "I did it right? Right?" He quietly asked.

Owen nodded, despite not truly knowing if he did it right.

Jack walked over to the computer. "Everyone ready?"

Everyone nodded again, though Owen was lying through their teeth. He wanted to get out of there quickly, but he wanted a few minutes to figure out what was going on. Owen felt sick to his stomach and his head started to pound.

"Ok." Jack pressed something on the computer and raced to sit in his chair.

Owen closed his eyes, tears falling down his face, as everything around him slowly went quiet.

Chapter 10

Jake felt weightless in the new environment. His feet touched something he could only think of as the ground. He looked around, panicked that he couldn't see anything or anyone at first. The whole place was black, reminding him of the ocean for some reason. He tried his best to keep himself calm as he whipped his head around the black space. Jake felt like he was spinning and falling the longer he looked around. Before his panicking started to get out of control, he saw Jack, then Theo, and finally Owen. Jake sighed after seeing Owen appear in the black space.

Owen looked around the space, scared and confused.

"Dude, this is the freakiest feeling in the world." Jake tried to break Owen out of his stunned state.

"This is the in between space." Theo was about to say something else, but got cut off by Jake.

"Can we fly?" Jake jumped up then slowly fell back down onto the invisible ground. "OHMYGOSH!" His voice echoed in the space. "THIS IS AWESOME!" He jumped again and attempted to do a backflip.

Jake watched Owen jump. "Woah." He gasped.

"I KNOW!" Jake still shouted with excitement. "Can we stay here forever?" He asked, jumping toward Theo. He tried to move in the air, flailing his arms like he was swimming. He moved a few inches, but it didn't keep him up in the air. Jake made eye contact with all of them as they watched him slowly float to the ground. Jake saw Owen attempt to hold back laughing.

Theo shook his head. "I don't know. But I don't want to figure it out." He finally answered.

Jake jumped up and out of the corner of his eye, he saw the white door thing Theo talked about. As he looked at it, Jake realized he kind of wanted to stay in this in-between space forever, where seemingly nothing can hurt them. In his defence, they were practically flying. This was the best place ever.

Jake jumped up into the air. "I bet I could jump higher than a house!" He exclaimed at the high point of his jump. He attempted to do the swimming thing again, but landed in the same position. Instead of getting up, he melted onto the floor.

"Yeah, me too." Owen agreed but quickly added. "Because houses can't jump."

"That's not what I mean and you know it!" Jake argued, offended, pointing a finger up at Owen.

Jack turned toward the light and without hesitating, started walking forward. "Let's get moving." He waved the group over.

"Awwwww!" Jake rolled onto his back and sprawled out on the floor. "But this place is awesome!" He whined.

Owen walked past him and Jake grabbed his ankle. Jake expected Owen to stop, but he kept walking.

"Nooooo! Stop!" Jake twisted to his stomach again

and let go of Owen's leg. "I'll get up." He pushed himself into the air and flailed around until his feet faced the ground. Owen watched, starting to tear up from holding back laughter. Once he landed, Jake sprinted up to Owen, who was only a few feet away.

"Calm down dude. We're not leaving you." Owen finally laughed, gently jabbing Jake in the side. Jake flinched slightly.

"Don't joke man, you were so far!" Jake draped an arm around him and leaned on Owen, trying to weigh him down. "I thought I was gonna lose you!" He wrapped his hands behind Owen's head and dramatically blinked at Owen.

Owen rolled his eyes and sighed. "If you keep acting like a big baby I might just have to." He jokingly admitted, holding the back of Jake's back.

Jake and Owen paused their walking for a moment, their expressions falling. They stared at each other, thinking about how they looked at that moment. Jake slowly let go of Owen, falling to the ground slowly, and Owen took a few small steps away from Jake.

"Nope." Owen mumbled, not looking at Jake as he walked forward stiffly.

"I don't even know what you're talking about man." Jake agreed, standing up quickly and keeping at least six feet between them.

They both heard quiet laughter in front of them, but they didn't address it. They walked in sludgy silence for what felt like days.

"I wonder what the real world's like." Owen broke the silence. "I wonder if it looks the same as the simulation." He looked over at Jake quietly walking beside him. "Maybe they have flying cars. That would be cool, right?"

"Yeah." Jake answered, but it took him a second to fully understand. "Wait, yeah, dude, that would be so cool! I bet it'll be like Back to the Future 2. That would be sick."

"Yeah man." Owen agreed. "We could get those skateboards they had."

"But we don't know how to skate."

Both of them kept walking, but their expressions froze in confused excitement.

"I didn't say we'd skate." Owen murmured, looking away.

"Then what's the point of having the skateboards?" Jake asked, getting in front of him and walking backward, laughing.

"I don't know dude, to look cool?" Owen laughed as he shoved Jake out of the way.

Jake froze for a second as he passed him. He thought for a moment before he tapped Owen's shoulder. "Tag! You're it!" He quickly jumped over Owen and started running. "Race you to the end!"

"You're so dead!" Owen raced after him.

Jake jumped over Jack and Theo, facing them. "Theo, Jack, when are we getting to the white blob?" He asked, using them as shields to dodge Owen while walking backward.

"Soon. It's not that far away." Theo explained, moving out of Owen's way. Jake quickly turned on his heel and raced off.

"Traitor! You like your own son more than me?!" Jake joked. Jake felt Owen right behind him, only a few inches away from tagging him. Jake looked past his shoulder, seeing Owen lunge forward, hurling through the air from the momentum. He jumped up to dodge Owen. Owen's body skidded on the ground before he quickly shot up.

"You can't stay in the air forever!" Owen shouted up to him. Jake flapped his arms up and down like a bird, thinking that was a good idea. Jake made a much slower descent with his crazy idea. He watched Owen leap up into the air after him. Jake resorted to his swimming method. Moving his feet out of Owen's reach, he very slowly moved across the black sky. Owen put his arms up, falling much quicker to the ground that way, then jumped up again. This time, he tagged Jake and grabbed his shirt.

"Awe man!" Jake exclaimed as Owen let go as he said.

"You're it!" Owen fell to the ground alongside Jake.

"You better start running then!" Jake tried to tag Owen before he ran off. He almost made contact but missed by a few inches. Jake sprinted off behind Owen, who constantly checked behind his shoulder. Jake was quickly closing the distance between him and Owen. He noticed how his body didn't hurt in the in between space. It made him feel great and free. Jake leapt at Owen, who almost didn't dodge in time. Owen jumped forward before Jake slammed into the ground where he was once standing.

"Hah! You missed!" Owen taunted before landing on his feet and running again.

Jake stood up quickly and charged behind Owen. "You're gonna wish I hadn't!" Jake taunted back.

Owen kept up his dodging and Jake kept up his running until his body started to hurt. It felt like he was walking up the stairs again. His leg muscles tightened and it was harder for him to keep up. Still, he kept trudging on closer to the white blob. They kept at it, Owen quickly maneuvering Jake's slow and poor timed attacks until Jake tripped over his own leg. He lost his balance completely and slowly face-planted into the ground. His whole body ached when he tried to pick himself up. Jake's arms shakily pushed him up off the ground, just enough for him to see Owen running toward him.

"What happened?" Owen quickly got to his knees. "I turned around and watched you fall."

Before Jake could answer, Jack and Theo were beside him. They helped him twist over to his back and held him upright.

"Are you dizzy? Hurting? Feeling sick?" Theo blurted out too quickly for Jake to respond.

"Yeah, I-I guess." Jake tried to catch his breath. "It just... hurts." He tried to explain.

Jack and Theo quickly started to bounce questions and ideas off of each other. Jake looked over at Owen, looking like he was going to explode with questions. Jake felt scared. Was this going to affect his ability to go to the real world? Will he be able to go at all?! So many questions and no answers.

"I can hold him up and we can cross together." Owen offered quietly, making Theo and Jack turn their heads.

"That won't work. The machine needs us to be apart to separate us into the right bodies." Theo explained, looking very sorry. "He'll need to cross by himself."

"Does it look like he can cross by himself!" Jack spat.

"At the very least, we can help him get to the door. We're only a few more feet away." Theo explained. When no one else tried to add anything, Theo threw Jake's arm over his shoulders. Jack helped stand him upright while Theo lifted them off the ground. Despite Jake's body hurting, it also felt limp. It was hard to move his legs forward because of the pain and sheer strength to use the muscles to move them. Jake felt weak and useless, at his utter low point. He hated this, not because of the pain he was causing himself, but the pain he was causing the others.

Owen went to his other side and helped hold him up. "Who's going first?" He asked.

"Jack and I will go first." Theo stated. "We'll make sure it is safe for you two to cross." Owen nodded.

After a few more steps, they were at the door. His body felt like mush, barely anymore pain because of how hard it was to feel and move everything. The last few steps they had to drag him over. Jake was placed down on the ground, very close to the door.

"Ok." Theo hugged Owen.

Jack beant down beside Jake. "I swear I'll make this right." He whispered to Jake. "You will be ok. I stand by those words." Jack finished talking to Jake before Theo was done saying his goodbyes to Owen, but Jack's words felt so touching to Jake. It made him want to cry, but he swallowed his tears.

"We'll see you on the other side." Theo let go of Owen, hesitated, but turned to the white door. He was the first to walk through. Jack turned to Jake, a tear finally escaping his eyes.

"Same here, boy." Jack mumbled, and slowly walked through.

Jake and Owen soaked in the silence for a moment. Their last time in the simulation. All their questions will be answered soon, all their pain and suffering will be over.

Jake saw Owen kneel down into his field of view. "I'm not going through until you go in." He whispered, barely holding back tears.

"Then we might be here a while." Jake joked, almost choking on his words. His eyes started to get swallowed with unshed tears as he struggled to roll himself over onto his stomach. Almost everything in his body felt numb and anything he could feel was painful as he tried to turn over. He tried using his arm, then his leg, but everything felt too weak and painful. What if he didn't make it through? What if his body was actually dead, and he was just about to kill himself going through? Jake started to quietly sob as Owen helped him roll over slowly, from his back to his side, then to his stomach. He then helped Jake get to his feet. No words were shared between them, the silence was all that was needed to show how scared, and worried, and anxious they were about this whole mess. Both of them were in tears, sobbing, when Owen hugged Jake to keep him upright.

"Owen..." Jake sputtered. "If I-... If I-..." He tried to get the words out, but they kept getting caught on something.

"Please. Don't say it." Owen begged, knowing where Jake was going. "Don't say it." He mumbled again, shaking his head.

"If I... don't... make it..." His words felt painful to himself, but they had to be said. "Please... please don't... be sad... or upset... I hate- I hate- ...seeing you that way." Jake smiled into Owen's shoulder.

"You're going to make it! I swear-! I swear-!" Owen choked on his tears, coughing before Jake continued.

"I'll always... I'll always be with you..." Jake

insisted, his throat trying to close up and stop working.

"But... but I- I need you!" Owen held him tighter.

Jake's lip trembled and his eyes started to hurt. "We should go." Jake swallowed. "Before- before... before Jack and Theo..."

Owen sniffed. "Promise me..." He mumbled, turning Jake's back toward the portal and letting go slightly. "That you'll... that you'll be-"

"You know... you know I can't- ... make that promise." Jake whispered.

Owen hugged him tightly. "See you over there." He mumbled. Then without another painful word, Jake was shoved through the portal by Owen.

Chapter 11

Owen opened his eyes to darkness. The sound of slow rhythmic beeping filled his ears before hearing a voice.

"Owen." The voice whispered into his ear, obviously Jake's. Owen jumped slightly but was stopped by something covering his face.

"Owen." He said again. "It's me, Jake..." He paused. "We... we didn't make it."

Owen's heart fell and his body slumped. "What?" He breathed.

Jake took a little while to respond. He sighed. "That's right." He told Owen. "I think we're still stuck inside..."

"Really?" Owen asked. He heard Jake let out a quiet snort, then take a deep breath.

"I think so... I mean, it's really dark" Jake said after obviously composing himself.

"It is?" Owen asked, somewhat buying what he was saying. Still, he tried to keep a straight face and tone.

"Phhh-!" Jake sputtered, then started to hyperventilate. It took him a long time to calm down. "Yes, really." He ended up saying.

Owen pushed himself upright, breaking the grip

of whatever was covering his eyes. The room was bright white, all the lights were on and blinding. Jack and Theo were in a corner, both of them turned away and pretended to do something else.

"Dude! That's just mean!" Owen blurted, now slightly leaning forward in the chair. Jake must have been behind him, because he didn't see him.

Jake laughed and Owen felt something lean on his chair. "Dude! You should have seen your face!" Jake cleared his throat and started to do an impression. "... really?" He whispered.

Owen turned around, looking at Jake. He then proceeded to stand up and point at Jake, slightly stepping away. "Dude! Your- your face!"

"What! What about my face!?" Jake felt his entire face.

"Your body! It's- It's- so hideous!" Owen exclaimed, continuing to step away and point a shaky finger at Jake. Jake looked down quickly but looked up quickly with scrunched eyebrows.

"Wait-." Jake got cut off.

"Jack! Theo! How could you not warn us that he was this disfigured!" Owen turned to Jack and Theo, who were both trying to hold back laughter. Their hands covered their mouths and Jack had to turn away to keep from breaking down.

"Dude!" Jake spat.

Owen fell back and leaned on the wall, weak in the knees. "You could scare children!" He kept pointing at Jake. Theo and Jack lost it, and Jake just stared unnamused.

It took Jack, Theo, and Owen a few minutes before calming down enough to start talking. Jack turned to the boys and walked over to them.

"If you boys are done messing around." Jack walked in between Owen and Jake. "We have some clothes for you." Owen looked down at what he was wearing. It was close to a hospital gown, but that was all.

"I'll take some." Jake walked over to Jack, who was kneeling beside two large backpacks that Owen had seen hikers wear.

"We don't give shoes, socks, or... undergarments." Jack whispered the last word as he reached into the bag. "Theo and I hope that these pants and shirts fit. Unless you want to-."

"I'll take pants!" Jake snatched a pair of black sweatpants Jack was holding out. He put them on under the hospital gown until Jack handed him a shirt. He threw the hospital gown onto one of the chairs and put on the white tee shirt.

"I'll take some too." Owen grabbed the last pair of sweatpants and the tee shirt. He took his time to put them on, but was so grateful to be completely covered in clothing instead of weird paper.

"Alright." Jack pushed himself off the floor. "We talked with a trusted work friend, Kyle. He said no one was supposed to come in this room today." Jack informed them. "We're hoping to leave when everyone's left for the day."

"When do we know when it's night?" Jake asked, walking closer to them.

"Our phone's work here." Jack pulled out his phone, showing them it was 3:59. "And this place shuts down at nine." Owen nodded and kept listening.

"So what is this place exactly?" Jake questioned.

"It's a movie and show making place." Theo explained, walking away from a door and its small square window. "But we work more like an animation company."

"Ohh, that makes sense." Jake nodded. "But then, what is this room?" He tried his best to gesture to the room.

"This..." Theo trailed off.

"This is your specific room." Jack cut him off. "You're the only people who have ever gone in and out of the simulation."

"Other than us." Theo added.

Owen sat down on the chair. "So we just sit here and wait?"

"Sadly, yes." Theo walked over to sit beside him.

"Does my mother know you both went in there?" Owen asked, cringing at calling the root of his problems, his mother.

Theo thought for a moment, but was cut off by someone entering the room. Jake and Owen fell to the floor, unsure what to do at that moment. Was it his mother? Was it one of the employees? Owen didn't know.

"Jack, Theo, you boys are in luck." The person spoke with enthusiasm. His footsteps got louder and the door shut. "We might be able to get the boys out of here earlier than we thought." Owen watched Jake stick his head up over the chair.

"Boys, this is kyle." Jack turned to Owen and Jake, introduced the older man. "You can get off the floor." He turned back to Kyle. "How?" He questioned.

"We have some college students coming to see what we do here. One of them is my niece" Kyle explained. "She could probably sneak them out if we ask." Once he was done, he turned to the boys. "It's nice to meet you two." He reached his hand out for Owen to shake. Owen hesitated for a second, having to process what he was doing, and shook Kyle's hand.

"It's nice to meet you too." Jake shook Kyle's hand without hesitation.

"Is your niece here?" Jack asked, trying to direct the conversation back. Owen sat back down on the chair and watched.

"Not yet." Kyle shook his head. "They're coming at five, I'll tell her then. And since I'm leading the tour, I'll just lead her to them."

"Perfect." Jack clasped his hands together, making a small sound. He turned to look at Owen and Jake, both sitting on the chairs.

"But what about you guys?" Jake asked.

Jack looked dead serious as he answered. "We're stopping this maniac." He stated and Theo shifted slightly, almost unnoticeably.

"And you're leaving us out of all that fun?" Jake joked, but was met with a scowl by Jack.

"This isn't fun." Jack told Jake harshly. "We might get into some serious legal trouble. We don't want you to be a part of that."

"So what will we do in the meantime?" Owen looked up at Theo when he asked.

Theo shrugged. "I'd say go with Kyle, but he's probably going to help us."

"Taking care of these boys is helping you." Kyle countered. "I'll do whatever you need."

"It's settled, you'll hunker down with Kyle while we sort this out." Jack noted, taking a step forward and sitting on the chair beside Jake. Owen saw Jake inch over slightly. He wondered if this was reminding Jake of his dad. Owen somewhat remembered Jake's father, he was an angry man and always serious. Jack was not all like him, but there were similarities.

"We just wait until five then." Kyle agreed. "I'll also tell her to drive you to my house. It's far from here, out in a rural area. The only thing we have out that way are cows." He explained.

"What happens if we're spotted? How will this work?" Jake looked over at Jack.

Jack thought for a moment. He stared forward as if trying to look for the answer behind the door. "You should call her and tell her to pick up some jackets or something for them." He finally spoke, but still didn't break eye contact with the door. "You'll put the hoods up over your heads and follow her straight out of the building. Lorietta doesn't come out of her office a whole bunch." Owen stared at Jack. Lorietta must be his mothers name. It was a weird, very unheard of name.

"She probably will for this tour." Kyle cut him off. Jack looked over at him. "She'll probably talk with the youth, see what they're interested in."

"Then we let the kids distract her." Jack told him. "Something, anything." He mumbled.

"What size are the boys?" Kyle asked while poking at his phone, probably calling or texting his daughter.

"I think they have extra-large shirts on now." Theo replied before Kyle pulled the phone to his ear.

"Hey sweet girl." Kyle answered. "Can I send you on an errand before you come over?" He walked over to a corner away from everyone.

"So far the real world's boring." Jake leaned forward and whispered to Owen.

"You mean you want to be chased by a monster?" Owen argued with a smirk.

"I just mean it feels slower." Jake answered. "You

102

know what I mean?" Owen sat there for a moment. He guessed he did. It was weird to figure out if things felt slow, but at the same time he started to get what Jake was saying.

"Two extra-larges, any size jacket-y thing with hoods." Kyle pulled his phone away from his ear and covered the bottom of it. "Would they like shoes?" He asked.

"Yes. Flip flops will be fine I think?" Theo turned to look at Jake and Owen. Owen nodded and Jake did the same.

Kyle put the phone up to his ear. "Can you also buy some flip flops? Size... let's go extra large." He waited for a response. "That's all, I'll repay you when you get here. Thank you. See you soon. Bye." He pulled the phone away from his ear and hung up.

"What time is it now?" Jake asked. Kyle looked down at his phone.

"It's almost 4:40. We have a little while." He walked over to them, but stayed standing.

"Do you boys have questions about anything?" Theo asked, looking over at Jake.

"How long were we in there for?" He asked. Theo looked like he was shaken to his very core.

"You were around ten or eleven when you went in?" Jack answered.

"That sounds right." Theo mumbled.

"So we've been in there for about... 5 or 6 years?!" Jake pointed out. "And you just now decided to get us out?"

Both of them went silent, but Kyle surprisingly answered. "Theo and Jack wanted you two to stay safe. The way Lorietta had them wrapped up, doing anything would have affected you." He told the boys. "They did what they could. Just four days ago they had an opening to go in there and get you out."

"fOUR DAYS!?" Jake exclaimed. Jack shushed him.

"Four days?" Jake said again, quietly this time.

"Time moves faster there." Jack explained. "Plus with the glitching nonsense, I guess it went even faster."

"We're still sixteen right?" Jake asked, and it made Owen start to think about it too.

"Yes, you're still sixteen." Jack sighed. "Time moved fast, aging was weird. You're out now, so we don't have to try and explain it to you."

"More like we don't have to figure it out." Theo told them.

Jake looked over at Theo. "One more question, I swear."

"Phht-!" Owen slapped his palms over his hands.

"What? What's so funny?" Jake asked, glaring at Owen.

"I bet you three bucks you'll ask another question within the next thirty seconds." Owen put it plainly.

"I don't ask a lot of questions." Jake looked over at Jack. Jack widened his eyes, in confused shock. He probably also thought that the answer was as clear as day.

"You do. You ask a lot of questions." Jack answered.

"Then this'll be the last one." Jake insisted, then proceeded to ask. "Why is... uhhhh... Lorietta! Why is she this way? Why did she make this place?"

"That's two questions." Owen informed him sarcastically.

Jake rolled his eyes. "If they answer one they'll answer the other. It doesn't count."

"The answers to those questions are... complicated." Theo hesitated. "She's a very intelligent person, she just uses it wrong."

"She either manipulates you and uses you, or she'll just blackmail you and use you." Jack told them simply. "Lorietta has money, influence, and dirt on everyone. If you cross her, she makes sure you disappear... one way or another."

"Sadly, yes." Theo nodded, his body hunched slightly. He looked down at the ground "Marrying her was because of manipulation, but staying with her was because of blackmail." He explained before jumping close to the topic. "The small bits she told me were about her parents being controlling. I know she was always running from one college to another, and I think she was trying to be a lawyer. I met her in some class for creative writing, all because we were paired up together for a project." He shook his head. "I guess she made this place just because she can. I remember her saying no one was taking her seriously about her technology... I don't know." He shrugged.

Jake sighed. "Ok." He slumped.

"I'm going to head out." Kyle walked over to the door. "Get ready for us in... about ten minutes?" He was about to walk out before he turned back around. "And just so you know, if all else fails." He patted his side, where Owen noticed a lump.

Jack nodded. "Sounds good." Kyle opened the door, looked around, then walked out. The door swung shut behind him, not making a sound.

"What was he talking about?" Jake asked.

Owen grinned, straightening his arm outward and pointed at Jake. "You owe me three bucks."

Chapter 12

Jake, Owen, Jack, and Theo sat there for probably more than ten minutes. In that time, Jake had to give Owen fifteen bucks. He was going into debt before having any money! He really did have a problem with asking so many questions.

The door cracked open and a redhead stuck her head inside. "Hello." She slipped in quickly and shut the door. "Are you all Theo, Jack, Jake, and Owen?" Jake spotted her large purse. It most likely had the rest of their clothing.

"That's us." Jack stood up and pointed to everyone as he introduced them. "I'm Jack. This is Theo, Owen, and Jake." Everyone stood up, Jake's feet freezing on the cold marble.

"It's nice to meet you all." She offered a sheepish smile. "I'm Virginia, but people call me Ginny."

"It's nice to meet you Ginny." Theo was the first to say something, leading Owen and Jake scrambling to say the same. She was very pretty. She had freckles all over her face, with bright green eyes.

"Everything you need should be in here." Ginny passed her purse over to them. Theo took it, took out two pairs of neon green flip flops, and two black sweatshirts.

"You two put these on." Jack quickly added. "And take off the tags."

Jake and Owen nodded, quickly slipping on the sweatshirts first.

"Did Kyle tell you the plan?" Theo asked, passing Ginny back her purse. Owen and Jake sat on the bed and pulled the tags off the flip flops.

"What Uncle Kyle told me was I have to take them back to his house." Ginny explained to Theo and Jack. "Just walk them right out the front door were his exact words."

"Yep. Our part of the plan is staying here to deal with her." Jack told her. "So if anything happens, just make your way back to us."

"Ok." Ginny nodded. "Are you two ready to go?" She asked.

Jake nodded. "Yep, just waiting on slowpoke here."

"I'm not slow!" Owen jumped up. Ginny giggled, eyes squinted as she covered her mouth with her freckle-covered hand. Jack narrowed their eyes at Jake and Owen.

"Calm down, we're not going to do it out there." Jake insisted.

Jack just rolled his eyes. "Be careful out there. Keep your heads down and your hoods up." He reminded them.

Theo hugged Owen. "You be safe too. We plan to be back at Kyle's by 10."

"Ok." Owen slowly hugged him back. Everyone walked to the door. Before Ginny could open it, Jack spoke.

"Follow Ginny. Never leave her sight. You two understand?" He said firmly.

"Who do you take us for?" Jake asked, then stomped his foot as Owen laughed. "It doesn't count! It was just a joke! You already have fifteen bucks of my imaginary money!" Ginny sighed, probably just now realizing how much of a handful they're going to be.

"Let's get going." She opened the door and let Jake and Owen out first. They started walking down the hallway before hearing a female voice ahead of them.

"And here we have our writers." The voice echoed.

"Turn the other way." Ginny murmured to them, gesturing quickly to turn. They started to walk the other way.

"Oh, hello." The voice was right behind them with college students murmuring. All three of them turned around. Jake kept his head pointed to the ground, but his heart pounded. Who stopped them? Was it Lorietta? Were they figured out? They only made it a few steps past the door. Were they seriously caught just now!?

"Hello, Ms. Lorietta." Ginny purposefully stepped in front of Jake and Owen. "I'm here visiting my uncle." Jake noticed how quick she was able to say that, and she actually sounded genuine.

"Hello, Ginny. Who are your friends behind you? Would you two be so kind as to take your hoods off?" Lorietta asked, sounding a little too nice. "It's a security measure. Someone should have stopped you from entering like that..." Her voice trailed off when they didn't comply. What do they do!? If they take them off, she'll know! If they leave them on, Jake didn't know what would happen.

"I'm sorry, they're very hard of hearing." Ginny answered for them. "They probably didn't hear you." Jake saw the back of Ginny's shoe, signaling that she took a step back. Was Lorietta coming closer? They're figured out, Jake knew it. He was trying his best to keep his breathing under control. Jake felt Owen press closer to him.

"Can you three give me a second." Lorietta told them, before she sounded like she was speaking in the other direction. Jake took a glance at the situation but Ginny motioned for him to put his head down and start walking the other direction. "Kyle, can you take the college students? Something important just came to my attention."

"Run." Ginny mumbled to them, and all three of them raced the few feet back to their door.

Theo and Jack jumped up from the chairs. "What happened?" Theo asked as Jack walked forward, shut the door, and shooed them away.

"Stay back." Jack told them, blocking the door with his body. Since the doors swung in and out, he had to stand facing the door and hold the handles in place.

"Lorietta was leading a tour of her own..." Ginny tried to catch her breath, shaking. "It was like she knew what was going on." As Ginny explained, Theo lifted a metal door open, revealing a plethora of tangled up wires. All three of them hunkered in the pile of wires. Theo stood in front of them, using his body as a wall. Owen and Jake let Ginny get in first. She kneeled down into the cords. Jake let Owen in next. He tried his best to get comfortable, not trying to be close to Ginny but still tried to get far in. Jake was last, trying to squeeze his body into the remaining space. It was a tight fit, saying the space was already small to begin with. Putting two teenagers in there only made it worse. Jake managed to squeeze himself beside Ginny.

"Stay put." Theo said quietly before shutting the door.

"Where do you think we're going?" Jake asked jokingly before it completely shut. It was dark, but surprisingly loud. The machine they were in hummed constantly and it beeped rhythmically. Jake felt claustrophobic and tied up thanks to the wires. He could barely see Owen and Ginny in front of them.

Jake wiggled and put his ear on a wall. He could hear everyone yelling, sometimes he could figure out words, but it was still garbled garbage.

"Are you getting anything?" Ginny asked quietly.

Jake shook his head before realizing she couldn't see him. "No." He whispered back.

"Are they here?" Lorietta's voice echoed through the chamber of wires and very little light came through the wires. Everyone went stiff and still. Jake held his breath.

"They aren't here you-." Jack's word was cut off by her slamming something.

"-Now!" Lorietta's word was loud, but wasn't the first one. It sounded very hostile and demanding. Owen, Jake, and Ginny inched closer together. Jake could feel everyone's bodies shaking. Jake could only imagine what was happening now. Did she have a gun? Why would she have one? Was she even going to use it if she had one? His thoughts kept spiraling and spiraling. She was going to find them. All this time getting out of the simulation just to die!

A shot fired.

"Show them! NOW!" Lorietta's shout was core-shaking yet crystal clear. Jake felt himself shrink and his panicked breathing was matched with everyone else's.

Ginny, Owen, and Jake hugged each other. Someone opened up their door halfway. It was Theo, his face was pale and tearstained despite tears still falling down his face. His movements were slow but jerky. Lorietta was right beside him, holding a gun to his head and moving him around.

"Finally..." Lorietta grinned, her voice soft. "My moneymakers." She jerked him backward and upright. "Up. Now." She stated harshly, her grin falling fast into a gritted frown. Owen got up first, though Ginny had to help him up. He wobbled when he got to his feet and Ginny had to steady him. Jake felt like he was hyperventilating and dying. What's going to happen now? Ginny got out next, somehow her movement was shaky but the closest to normal. Jake was next. He pushed himself up to all fours and tried his best to crawl out. His vision was blurred with tears. They were caught and no one knew what was going to happen next. He needed help from the door to stand up.

"You." She pointed a finger at Owen, but her hand didn't leave Theo's neck. "And you." She then pointed at Jake. "Chairs." Jake and Owen stumbled to the chairs. As Jake sat down, he saw Jack. He was up with his hands on his head in a corner. His eyebrows were scrunched but his eyes were red and teary.

"Pick up the two wires on the floor." Lorietta told them, walking around to be in between both chairs. Both of them quickly complied, Jake fumbled around with the wires. He stuck one in each hand.

"Put them on." Lorietta shoved Theo to the side, but pointed the gun at him with both hands. "If you so DARE to move!" She snapped at him. He pushed his back against the wall and shook his head violently. "Good."

She smiled, but her eyes were still narrowed and glaring. She turned to the brick of technology to the left of Jake. Lorietta looked at Owen, then to Jake. Her face was contorted in anger, but she still had a present smile. It made her look terrifying.

The smile faded quickly as it appeared. "I said, PUT THEM ON!" She spat through gritted teeth and her hand holding the gun by her side tightened. Jake flinched and quickly put the wires by his temples, not fussing with what color was on which side.

"Ginny..." Lorietta grumbled, stepping around the chairs again and over to her. Ginny became wide-eyed, shrinking slightly the more Lorietta came closer. She stared at Ginny, looking her up and down. "I have no need for any witnesses." She muttered. Ginny flinched when Lorietta moved her arm up slightly. "Unless..." She took a step forward and moved her face closer to Ginny's with every word. "You do this one, simple, task."

"Anything." Ginny mumbled, her mouth barely moving when she spoke.

Lorietta moved her face back and pointed to the machine between Jake and Owen. "Active the machine." Jake made eye contact with Ginny, trying to tell her through his eyes to just do it. They can just come back out. This won't stop them. Unless, the machine wipes their minds. They wouldn't remember anything when they went in. What would happen to them when they went in?

Lorietta moved Ginny's face to look back at her. "Answer little girl. Die or activate the machine." She stated. "I think the answer is quite clear." She put a hand on her chest. "So what is it?"

Ginny froze up. "I-... I-I-."

"Answer NOW child!" Lorietta shouted as Ginny gasped.

"The machine!" Ginny nearly cut Lorietta off.

Lorietta smiled. "Good choice." She said smugly. She moved out of the way and gestured for Ginny to move forward. Ginny drug her feet forward, around Jake's chair, and over to the machine.

"It's very simple." Lorietta told her quietly. "You just press the red button."

Ginny stared down at the panel, then looked over and Owen and Jake. She jerked her head away, closing her eyes. She sighed and opened her eyes. Ginny lifted her arm, inching it closer and closer to the red button. Jake turned his head and closed his eyes, unable to see what happened next.

"EVERYONE FREEZE!" A loud voice echoed around the small room. Jake's eyes shot open. Lorietta flinched to the loud voice. It was Kyle, his hands were up and wrapped around a gun of his own.

"Drop the gun, Lorietta." Kyle's eyes glared at her. Lorietta hesitated. "NOW! DROP IT NOW!" He snapped. Lorietta's gun clattered to the ground. Jack and Theo walked around her as Kyle walked forward through the room. Lorietta walked backward, her hands above her head. Kyle moved her gun behind him, and to Jake's surprise, Theo picked it up. Theo fumbled with it but quickly aimed it at her.

Lorietta kept backing up until her back hit the wall. "Kyle, Kyle. This is a huge misunderstanding." She didn't tremble. She didn't look afraid. Her voice didn't even crack when she spoke. She sounded calm, eerily calm.

"Don't worry Lorietta. This will be your last

misunderstanding." Kyle nodded, demanding his incision. He walked past Ginny, grabbing and holding her close with one arm, and still held the gun straight at Lorietta with the other.

"Oh, I don't think so." She shook her head, grinning.

"Oh. I think so." Kyle walked past Jake's chair.

Jack walked over and helped him up out of the chair, grabbing him close. Jake sobbed into his chest, Jake felt Jack start to walk, so he went with him to stand behind Kyle. Owen was attached to Theo when they walked over but quickly jumped on Jake when he got close. Jake turned to hug Owen and Owen hugged Jake. Both of them looked up to watch Lorietta.

"You're either going to come with us willingly or die. Your choice." Kyle stated.

"If I die, all of you would be to blame." Lorietta insisted. "His fingerprints are on that gun." She was talking about Theo. "There are no cameras in here, and there are no witnesses. You're screwed." She pointed out.

"KIDS!" Kyle shouted. Jake and Owen turned their heads to see two male college students walk in, their phones out and recording.

"I knew what you were doing, Lorietta. So I asked someone on security to take the rest of the college students outside." Kyle explained. "I had these two stand outside and record everything."

Now Lorietta looked scared. Her eyes went wide and her hands went up. "Ok... now this is bad. You don't want to do this..." She smiled nervously, walking forward. Lorietta looked at Theo. "Sweetheart, please!" She asked.

Jake watched Theo step forward, his arms shaking with either fear or anger. Maybe it was both. "No." He said. "I'm done. I want to keep my son, his friend, everyone, safe from you."

BANG!

Theo pulled the trigger and Lorietta collapsed to the floor, blood trickling from the left side of her chest. His arms fell, the gun fell from his hands, then he fell to the floor on his knees. Everyone was silent for a good while before they heard Theo whisper.

"She's gone. It's over."

Jake wasn't sure if Theo was upset or happy until he heard him laugh slightly. He picked himself off the floor. He raced over, picked up Owen and twirled him around in the air in a hug.

"We're safe and sound. And with this evidence, we prove our innocence in this whole thing!" Theo exclaimed, placing Owen on the ground.

Everyone was still shaken, sweating, and adrenaline spiked, but now they can finally relax. Their running was over. They're finally done.